Like a LIKE A **Memory**

ABBI GLINES

#1 *NEW YORK TIMES* BESTSELLING AUTHOR

To *Emerson Pearce Sullivan*. I didn't know my heart was missing a piece until I held you in my arms.

To my readers,

When I completed the Sea Breeze series I knew one day this story would be told. However, I imagined it being many years from now. When I completed the Rosemary Beach series I knew it was going to be sooner than I expected.

Nate Finlay and Bliss York were in my head. I could hear their voices and their story was unfolding. I began to get excited thinking of returning to the characters and places of two of my bestselling series. Especially joining the two with their children.

If you haven't read Sea Breeze or Rosemary Beach that's okay. You don't have to. This book stands alone. Those who do know the backstory, I hope it's all you dreamed it would be. I loved every moment I spent returning there.

Abbi

LIKE A
Memory

Prologue

❤ BLISS YORK ❤

I WAS SAVED. After three days without Eli, who was at basketball camp, Larissa came and rescued me. She was taking me to the beach to stay with her for the rest of the week. No more feeding the chickens and gathering the eggs or organizing the barn with daddy. That was the worst. I was getting a farmer's tan and I wanted the kind of tan a bikini line was involved in.

Eli called yesterday and I told him how boring things were. I was fifteen. This summer was supposed to be fun. Not like all my other summers. Helping daddy on the farm was no longer exciting for me. I told Eli this and the next thing I knew his Aunt Larissa who was three years older than us called me. I owed him big.

Larissa would be leaving to go away to college in the fall. But for now she still lived at home with her parents, which were Eli's grandparents. They had a big fancy house on the beach with a pool that was to die for. I couldn't wait. Momma agreed I could go. I'd asked her pleading on my knees while I handed her the phone when Larissa called to ask. Of course, she had to talk to Larissa's mom but in the end she said "yes" and here I was. Standing on the white, sugar sand beaches of Sea Breeze, Alabama. It was full of tourists and boys with tanned bodies and it smelled like the ocean and coconut oil and I loved it. Loved it! This was what I'd dreamed my summer would be filled with. Now I was here and living this life.

I owed it all to Eli and I would find a way to thank him. He loved my chocolate chip cookies. But those seemed inadequate. He deserved more for this rescue. Maybe I would talk to my dad about taking Eli fishing. He got along with my brothers and he liked to go fish in the summer at our hunting camp. My dad and brothers never hunted but they loved to fish. Eli wasn't one for shooting the deer either but he also loved to fish.

Larissa was flirting with the lifeguard and I couldn't blame her. He was very attractive. Smiling at the idea of finding someone my age to flirt with I put down my towel and took off my cover up. The hot pink bikini I had on covered more than what most of the girls wore out here. A lot more than Larissa's. But it was all my daddy would approve of and getting him to approve of this one had almost been impossible.

I thought about putting in my earbuds, listening to music and enjoying the view. But then I changed my mind. I liked the sound of the waves and people surrounding where I lay. I pulled *Pride and Prejudice* out of my bag. This would be my sixth time to read it. Hands down this was my favorite book.

Just as I was about to finish chapter two a shadow fell over me. I figured it was Larissa. Looking up I grinned, about to ask if she had herself a hot date. My eyes locked on a familiar face. One that was older, a face I remembered, from two long summers ago. A face a girl would never ever forget. His silver eyes were stunningly breathtaking.

He was sixteen now but his muscular bare chest looked at least eighteen. I hoped Larissa didn't see him. Her tiny bikini and D cup boobs would draw his attention real fast.

"Bliss," he said, remembering my name.

"Nate," I replied as I sat up. I'd day dreamed about him often since that meeting on the beach when I was thirteen years old.

He smirked like he was impressed. Like he expected me to remember him but wasn't positive I would.

"I was beginning to wonder if you still lived around here." He spoke then moved to take a seat beside me. He made it look sexy and cool, just like I remembered from that summer. He wasn't awkward, didn't weirdly squat, like most people do in the sand.

"You've looked for me?" I asked. My heart doing a happy flutter in my chest. He had actually wanted to find me.

"Of course I did. You're my favorite memory about this place. Sure as hell ain't my grandpop's bar."

He cursed. Eli never cursed. My brothers did when my parents weren't listening, but they didn't do it in public. When they were out having to work on the farm they would curse for the sake of cursing. The way Nate did it seemed much older. Like he was sure of himself.

"How long are you in town for?" I asked specifically wanting to appear as cool as Nate did with his cursing. Though inside I felt something else. I was like a silly little girl that wanted to squeal that he was here. That my dream guy had returned to Sea Breeze.

"All summer. My parents think I need a break from Rosemary Beach and my friends. In other words, I'm being punished."

"Punished?" I asked from fascination.

He grinned then winked at me. "A story for another time. No need to scare you off. Hell, I just found you."

Scare me off? Hardly. I wasn't going anywhere. In fact, I would sit in this spot all summer and refuse to leave if it meant Nate Finlay would be by my side.

Chapter One

♥ BLISS YORK ♥

SEVEN YEARS LATER . . .

SENIOR PROM. I didn't go to mine. Much like everything else in high school. I missed it all. It wasn't until I turned nineteen that I went on my first real date. The only experience I had with boys until then was one summer when I was fifteen. I spent it with a boy. One I'd never forget. He was like everything else in my life that had been good . . . before the cancer.

In late October after he'd returned to Rosemary Beach, Florida, I began experiencing fatigue with a fever. Neither could be explained. By November both were out of control and I was then diagnosed with leukemia. My world changed in one visit, that consultation with the doctor and my family. And the boy I thought I loved was put away in my memory to adore. When I was scared, I brought him to mind, which back then was way too often.

I didn't answer his calls or respond to his texts and around Christmas he gave up trying. What would I say to him? The idea of that boy seeing me hairless with all the side effects of chemo would ruin those special memories of the summer we had together. So, I preserved them yet in return lost him. Everything soon became all about surviving each day. Beating the darkness of the cancer that ravaged my physical body. In the end, I won.

Yes, I have beaten cancer. However, since my mother lost her father to cancer, my mother continues to hover over me. She can't allow me to live normally although I've been cancer free for almost four years now. Dad said to "be understanding." My mother was terrified when I was first diagnosed. She cried a lot back then and held me. I often wonder if I fought so hard to beat it because I didn't want my momma to hurt. I couldn't stand the idea of how she'd suffer if she lost a child.

Now here I was at twenty-two, still living at home taking photos of the oldest of my three younger brothers Cruz. Snapping photos of him with his date to the prom. Living through watching him was something I was accustomed to. Although I was ready for that to change. I was glad my brothers had normal lives and I'd been able to experience the normalcy I lost by observing them. Cruz had done all the things I hadn't been able to do during my bout with leukemia.

Watching my momma and daddy, especially momma, being parents to healthy kids was nice and I loved to see it. The boys gave up a lot during those years that my sickness owned our family. They had to stay with my parents' closest friends, Willow and Marcus Hardy. Mom and dad had lived with me, at the Children's Hospital in Atlanta.

Cord was now sixteen. Our parents had missed his tenth birthday because I was going through chemo that day. Clay had turned eight that very same year and they'd also been absent for that. I was lucky the boys weren't bitter. The leukemia didn't only rob my teenage years, but it also stole many of their memories. Memories my parents should've been a part of. Instead, the boys made me cards, sent me boxes filled with magazines and books, along with cookies they made with Willow.

Finally, as a family, we'd come into balance. We were mostly normal now. As I took the last photo of Cruz and watched momma kiss his cheek, I could smile and know everything was okay. I was here to see my brothers grow. My life wasn't cut short like I'd feared. I was given a second chance. I'd missed a lot and it was time I stopped missing. Momma didn't need to hover anymore. I was healthy and I was an adult. I'd stayed home to keep her happy. Now it was time for me to live the life I should have been living. The one I had held off on for my momma's sake. I knew dad would understand. He'd be sad but he'd get it. However actually telling them I was moving out wasn't going to be easy.

"Drive careful," dad called to Cruz. He was taking Dad's new blacked out Jeep and dad really loved that Jeep. This was one of the many ways my parents tried to make it up to the boys. They knew they'd missed a lot of their life because of me. So, they tried to make what they weren't missing extra special.

"Have fun! Text me photos!" my mother yelled to them as they left. As if Cruz would be taking pictures and texting them to his mother. I tried not to smile, but failed, the idea was funny to me.

"Mom, he won't be taking any pics." Cord broke it to her with a roll of his eyes before momma turned around and grinned. "I know. I said it to Christina. She will. She'll be glad to."

Christina was his date and girlfriend. They'd been together for about three months. This was a record for him. My brother went through girls like crazy. Christina he called his "girlfriend." This was a first for Cruz.

Hadley Stone was his long running torch. She was a year older than Cruz and the daughter of a rock star, who happened to be friends with my parents. Jax Stone had been a major teen idol back when my dad was in college. He was now a rock legend, though he married one woman, and stayed with her all these years. They raised two daughters together, their stability making him popular, because usually it was the other way around.

Hadley, however, was different. She had been sheltered because of Jax's fame and she wasn't very social. Every time we had a get together with my parents' group of friends Cruz would constantly flirt with Hadley. It was comical and a little sad. She wasn't interested in the least.

Cruz typically got any girl he wanted. He looked just like dad at that age. Momma said he was the spitting image of daddy. But Hadley wasn't impressed. It was good for him I guess. Cruz had an ego Hadley kept in check. He needed that to keep him grounded.

"I'm going to the movies with Hendrix." Cord headed for the old blue Ford truck that he shared with Cruz on a schedule.

"I thought y'all had been banned from the theatre," momma reminded him.

Cord glanced back over his shoulder. "Not the one in Mobile. Just Sea Breeze."

"Don't get into trouble," dad said, in his stern and fatherly voice.

Hendrix Drake and Cord couldn't go anywhere and not get into trouble.

"Good luck with that," I replied.

Momma looked at me concerned. "Those Drake boys are a mess."

I laughed, in my opinion, that's the pot calling the kettle black. People said the same about the York boys. Momma's boys were as bad as the Drake's. It's why my best friend Eli Hardy and I have been referring to the Drake's and my brothers as "the terrible six," since shortly after their births.

"I need to talk to y'all while the boys are gone," I then told mom and dad. My youngest brother Clay was staying the night with Keegan Drake. I needed to take this opportunity to tell them I'd be moving out. Next week was closing fast.

"Okay," momma replied, studying me closely now.

Dad added "can we talk over dinner?"

"Sure," I said. "That's fine." It wasn't going to be easy either way, with or without food didn't matter.

"What's this about? Are you feeling okay?" Momma suddenly looked terrified. She lived with the fear of my resuming sickness and I wished she wouldn't.

"I feel great. It's not that."

"You look a little pale," she said, putting her hand to my forehead.

"Momma, I'm fine."

This was why I had to leave. She'd always treat me like this. The sick little girl who she had to take care of and protect.

"If you think you're getting sick we need to see a doctor . . ."

"Momma, I'm not sick," I interrupted her again.

"Are you sure?"

"I'm moving out."

They both suddenly froze. Neither had a response.

~NATE FINLAY~

OCTAVIA'S? SERIOUSLY? OCTAVIA'S? She was naming it after herself. I wondered why this surprised me. Octavia was brilliant and had also been blessed with a dose of creativity. A generous one I admit. But she was also the only child of the Beckett Department Store founder. Much like myself Octavia was privileged, born into wealth and raised with advantage, although hers affected her differently.

This was why my mother was not happy about me announcing

our engagement. Mom didn't care for Octavia. She said she wanted for me what she and dad had but that wasn't going to happen. Mom thought I would have that with Lila Kate. I knew what they were all thinking. They had my wedding planned and booked the moment Lila Kate was born. When they found out Lila Kate was a girl they all started planning it in their heads. Sure they didn't say it but they sure as hell thought it. The whole damn bunch even if they don't admit it. Octavia wasn't Lila Kate. Not by any stretch of the imagination.

The problem with Lila Kate was we thought of each other as family. She was just like another little sister. She knew it and felt the same way. Our mothers, however, were still holding onto hope and believing we could still get married. That we would magically come together.

Octavia fit me. We were more alike than my mother realized. We both wanted to make our own mark on the world separate from our well-known parents. We wanted to travel and didn't want kids. She was a touch spoiled. No, actually Octavia was ruined, but we'd agreed to sign prenup agreements to protect both of our interests.

What my parents had was rare. You didn't find a lot of them out there in this world anymore. Sure, I'd grown up around family and friends that lived in similar circumstances and had great marriages. But I wasn't like them or their children. I didn't want to settle down in Rosemary Beach, breed and raise my offspring. Neither did I desire afternoons filled with golf followed by dinner at the Kerrington, the elite country club in town. I wanted to chase a life that I didn't know and depend on myself for a living. I wanted to be my own man.

I shoved those thoughts aside. That was the life my mother wanted for me. Not the one I wanted and she knew it. She'd respect it. Time to focus on what I needed to do. I was here to get Octavia's shipment moved in while she was in Rome buying more. Her grand opening was two weeks away. There was a lot to be done in fourteen days and I had a feeling I was going to be stuck. The only positive was I'd have time with my grandpop while doing this shit for Octavia. My mom's dad owned a restaurant in Sea Breeze, Alabama where the first *Octavia's* was opening. Next month the tourists would come and she wanted to be ready for them.

I pulled the keys to her store from my pocket and headed for the seaside location. Of course, her store was right in the most expensive part of the strip. Grandpop's place wasn't anything like this. It was far from the higher end, brand new construction. His place had character that didn't overwhelm you. Octavia's business had polish and flair, but it didn't have a history like grandpop's.

The door to Octavia's swung open and out stepped a tower of boxes. I stopped, because the tower was tipping towards me, and just before it crashed I spoke.

"Careful," I said, before reaching to steady the body behind the cardboard. "Can you see where you're going?"

A heard a squeal and then they came down. I moved to help when my eyes locked with a pair I knew all too well. I'd only seen eyes like that once before and they were blue and deep and cool. The long thick dark hair tumbling down past her shoulders was also familiar to me. She was older and her body now curved in all the right places. She had definitely developed since the teenage years. No longer fifteen she'd become a woman.

Bliss York had been my first love. Or so I'd thought back then. Come to find out she'd been my first lust, because I had no idea how to love. Her face could stop traffic and that was without any makeup. She was as natural as I remembered. Nothing fake about her. Her smile had once made everything perfect in my world.

"Oh, I'm sorry . . ." she said, trailing off as her eyes scanned my face. I saw the realization there. She remembered me. Knew who I was. The boy who had given her that first kiss. Told her he would love her forever. Then I left after a summer of what I thought was the beginning of forever. I'd been a bit of a dreamer back then. It was before I realized that women weren't as soft and pretty on the inside as they were on the outside. My mother was perfect, inside and out, but my little sister Ophelia had a definite evil streak.

"You work here?" I asked before she could say my name. I didn't want to remember that summer. I had remembered it for far too long. Once I finally got it through my head that Bliss York wasn't the perfect girl, I'd let myself forget her entirely.

She opened her mouth to speak, then slowly nodded her head.

I knew that Octavia had hired someone to help her get things ready. I just hadn't been told her name. Not that it mattered. That was seven summer's back and a part of my past that would stay there.

I picked up a fallen box. "I'm Octavia's fiancé Nate." That should answer her questions and also lead her to believe I didn't remember. "I'll get these boxes to the recycle bin."

I didn't wait for her to give me her name. I went to work picking up the rest of the fallen boxes. She didn't move for what felt like several minutes, but was just a few fleeting seconds. I was tense. Not sure why. If she told me who she was and asked if I remembered, I could still act as if I'd forgotten. Seven fucking years had passed. We'd been kids then. We weren't now. I was a different person and I was sure she was too.

"Okay, um . . . thank you," she said. I wanted to look up and watch her go. To take in the woman she'd become. To see just how much her body had changed. The glimpse I'd allowed myself at first had been impressive and I wanted another. She had been a beauty back then. Now she was gorgeous and I had to fucking work with this beauty for the next two weeks.

Shit.

This would only happen to me.

I turned to walk off with the boxes when the door opened back up.

"I'm sorry. I forgot to tell you where the recycle bin is located." She sounded formal, nervous and unsteady. I could ease her worry by just being honest and clearing the air right now. But that meant I had to remember her. The girl I'd purposely forgotten. I'd told her I loved her and she had been the only girl I'd ever said that to. You live and learn in life and I'd lived and learned with Bliss York.

I have to stop musing on this shit.

"It's just behind the building there," she pointed.

I nodded. "Got it." Then I walked off. I didn't make eye contact. I didn't even thank her.

"Do you need help?" she called out.

"Nope." I was being an ass. That was the only way to handle this. My momma would be ashamed.

Chapter Two

NATE FINLAY. HOW did this happen to me? Not that it was going to be an issue because he didn't even remember who I was. Which stung. Bad.

Thoughts of him were what got me through some of the hardest times of my life. When I was sick after chemo I would focus on our summer and the times we had together. Thinking about that helped me forget the hell I was living through.

And still, he didn't remember me. Had no idea who I was.

Well, I was healthy now. Stronger. I no longer needed his memory to get through the day. I guess if I had to be slapped in the face with a grown, ridiculously good-looking Nate Finlay who had no idea who I was, then this was a good time. I could handle it.

I slowly turned from the window of Octavia's store where I had watched him walk away with the boxes. Nate Finlay was engaged to Octavia, who had given me my very first job. I liked her without really even knowing her. My first impression was that she was nice. I was looking forward to working with her. More like *for* Octavia, since she owned the store. Maybe a little less now that Nate was in the picture. But it was good. I was here and on my own.

No one would remember Nate but Eli. I'd told him about Nate that summer. He had listened to me talk, although I knew he didn't care, not the way a female would. I just didn't have a lot of those. Not like Eli. I was closer to him than anyone else on earth. Larissa knew some about him simply because she'd been the reason I had been at the beach that summer. Then the few friends I had that would have seen me with him wouldn't remember from that long ago. At least I hoped not.

Tonight, Eli would help me finish moving my things into the apartment we now shared. I could tell him. I had to tell someone. Maybe talking about it would help me close the door on my past with Nate that summer. Then again, it might make it worse.

My phone vibrated in my pocket. Eli had sent me a text. I swear we were on the same wavelength. It was like he knew I had a problem without me telling him I had a problem.

"You good?" was all he sent.

"Yep." I replied. Simply stalling. No reason to get into this now. We had a bottle of wine and a lot of work tonight and that would be the time for discussion. I'd tell him about it then. At least we would have something to talk about while we were moving my things in.

The door opened and I knew it was Nate. I didn't turn to look. I continued lifting the clothing from the box I'd positioned in front of me. I needed to finish today's inventory before other shipments arrived.

"Anymore trash?" he asked.

I put a smile on my face before straightening to look Nate in the eyes. "That's all. I'll have more later."

He nodded without eye contact. Again, it made no sense. He'd done the very same thing outside. Was there something on my face or in my nose? I'd eaten a protein bar for breakfast.

Maybe nuts had gotten in my teeth?

I quickly went back to unpacking.

"Octavia left me with a list of things she needs done. I'll go back to the office to begin." He said it like a question but he ended it like a statement. I nodded. Didn't say anything. What was the point in responding?

When I was sure he was out of the front of the store I stood up and sighed with relief. That was awkwardly painful and he didn't even know it. The summer we had been together he was attentive, very different. Not like the man he had become. This guy I didn't know at all. I guess we all change with age and time. I had just hoped that the memory I had of Nate would remain untouched. But reality was ruining it.

The next two hours flew by. Nate stayed in the back working on the list Octavia left for him. I finished organizing like she had instructed when Octavia called this morning. More things would be arriving this afternoon. I needed to be ready to receive them.

While I looked for something else to do the door opened which spun me around. I began to say "we're not open yet," but I stopped when I saw it was Eli. He had two brown bags and a smile.

"I brought food," he said. "Lots of it." I knew without asking that he had my favorite burger from The Pickle Shack in the bag.

"You're my hero, Eli. I'm starving." I wouldn't stop working as long as Nate was here. Not to leave and go get food. I wasn't sure if he'd be reporting to Octavia. If he was, good things needed to be said, because this job was important to me.

"I took a wild guess and didn't think you'd leave work to get food on your official first day."

"That's why you're my favorite person on earth." I loved The Pickle Shack.

Eli walked over to the empty counter and put the bags down gently. "This whole place looks breakable."

"Eli, paper bags won't hurt it."

"Good because it's time to celebrate with some greasy ass burgers. You have a job and you are officially independent as of tonight."

He wasn't a big fan of the greasy burger. I knew Eli wouldn't eat one. He'd have their grilled chicken sandwich. Eli was a fanatical health nut. He ran six to ten miles a day and ate "clean" as he called it, which did amazing things for his body. There was always some beautiful woman on his arm or attempting to lock onto his arm. I tended to get in the way sometimes and I hated that for Eli. We'd fought about this more than anything else because he enjoyed using me as an excuse. A means to free himself from women. Or I suppose I saw it that way. I didn't want to be a crutch that prevented my friend from falling in love in the future. For some reason, he was scared of that. The idea terrified him.

He had parents like mine, happily married, and he'd grown up in a stable environment. There wasn't any reason for him to be damaged or be fearful of a real commitment. But he was. To an extreme.

"I know you aren't eating a burger."

He'd placed mine directly in front of me.

He raised his eyebrows. "Hell yeah I am! We're celebrating."

"You hate greasy food."

"You love it, so we," he then motioned with his hand, sweeping it back and forth, "are eating to quicken our deaths, by clogging and sealing our arteries."

I loved Eli. I wasn't in love with Eli. I loved him the way I loved my brothers. Once I thought I could love him another way, but we were young. Nate Finlay had walked into my life. After that my sickness and fighting to live, changed everything for me. During that time Eli had cemented himself under the title of "world's best friend." He'd seen me at death's door. Been there when I fought back. Eli was with me through it all.

~NATE FINLAY~

SHE WAS IN there with a guy. I stood outside the storage door listening to them laughing and talking. I should have figured she'd be in a relationship. A girl like that doesn't stay single. The fact it annoyed me was stupid. But damn, it bothered me. She had remained in my memory as mine. Even though time had passed and we had grown up. She didn't seem to have changed much either. Other than the fact the girl I thought to be beautiful was now undeniably breathtaking.

We'd spent a fucking summer together seven long years ago. Bliss was no longer that innocent girl I'd given her first kiss to. Not anymore. She was a grown ass woman. Preserved in my memory was a girl. Though that was definitely a woman in there.

Maybe that was what was so aggravating. I liked having her in my memory as that perfect girl to unveil and remember as unblemished. I wouldn't have that to cherish anymore. She'd be in my world from day to day and I would see her imperfections. The young girl was gone and so was her sweet innocence. Life did that to everyone.

I'd kept myself from walking in there to remind her that her lunch was only an hour. That would make me look like a bastard. I had no reason to be. She had worked nonstop since I had arrived and she was due a fucking break.

"Did you get the rest of your things packed up? Are they ready to move this evening?" The guy asked with a casual familiarity that bothered the hell out of me. What the fuck was wrong with me?

"Yep. Momma cried while I was doing it. Just about killed me to hear it. I've heard her cry too much. It was the hardest part.

She wasn't sobbing, just tearing up. I let her hug me and tell me she loved me. That she wanted this for me. She was working through her emotions. She trusts you to take care of me. As if I needed any protection."

Bliss sounded somewhere between annoyed and amused.

"She's going to worry, B. You know that. Can't expect her not to."

Bliss sighed. "Yeah. I get it. I just wish we could move on from it. You know? Forget it. Try being normal."

They were quiet for a moment while I tried to figure out what the hell that meant, trying "normal?" Why couldn't Bliss try normal? From what I remembered she was very normal.

"It's only been four years," the guy responded. "She's gonna need more time than that. That's like a day to a mother, B. To her you're still an infant. In many ways you've just been born."

Again, Bliss sighed. "I know."

Four years since what? What happened? I felt guilty for eaves-dropping, but now I was curious. I wondered if Octavia knew what they were talking about. Not that I would ask her. It wasn't my business. I shouldn't have listened in.

I bumped into a broom backing away from the door. It hit a dustpan and both went to the floor with a crash. I winced and froze.

"What was that?" Eli asked.

"Octavia's fiancé," she replied. "Guess he must've dropped something."

She didn't call me by name or tell him anymore. Instead she started in on painting. The color her new bedroom would be in the apartment the two were sharing. She had a different bedroom than his? It made me question who he was. Were they intimate? Why the hell was I fixated on this?

I started to walk away and stop being nosey when she said his name out loud. Bliss said "Eli" and I knew who he was. She'd told me about "Eli" seven years ago. He wasn't her boyfriend. He was her closest friend. I had been jealous until she explained it. They were much closer than any relationship I'd ever had with a girl in my life. Even Lila Kate. I soon learned that they were exactly what she said and Bliss York hadn't been lying.

Just friends.

And they still were.

I left them to their conversation and went out the back door to my truck. I needed something to eat. An escape. To get the hell away from Bliss. I'd think it through then put it behind me.

I pressed Octavia's number on my phone. Talking to her would remind me of the life I now lived. And why it fit me. Why Octavia fit me perfectly. And why Bliss York never would. That's what I was telling myself. I didn't know the woman Bliss York had become. I didn't know anything about her at all.

"Hey, make it fast," she said. "I'm getting off the plane in Milan. The buyer that took me to Rome convinced me I had to come here. Don't have much time to talk."

Octavia, she was all business. Straight and to the point. She wasn't dramatic or needy. That was what every man needed. I'd seen enough drama from my sisters and even my mother at times. My dad had the patience of a saint. As for me, I didn't. Drama and women were more than I could handle. Octavia didn't inspire drama. She was too busy making her life appear perfect. I fit into her role and she fit into mine. It worked.

Chapter Three

♥ BLISS YORK ♥

M OST GUYS WHO had their own place would live in filth. Not that I'd ever seen another guy's apartment. But I did have three brothers and knew what their bedrooms looked like. When momma had enough she would threaten them, often within an inch of their lives, then they quickly put their rooms in order.

Eli wasn't like that. He was clean, tidy and neat. He had a place for everything. I was a little worried that I wouldn't be able to keep things as clean as he wanted them. I wasn't as tidy as he was. I never mentioned it because Eli would lie and tell me it's okay, that my comfort was most important. Which we would both know was not true. Even a small mess would drive him nuts.

I watched him put the last box in my new bedroom. The smile on his face matched mine. It had taken longer than we'd both planned but we were here now getting started. Living on our own like we'd always planned. Eli moved out when he began college and got a job to support himself. I often wondered when I could join him. When our brothers and sisters were driving us nuts we'd planned this very thing. Being roommates and living on our own.

I had just beaten cancer when he left. It was too soon for me. I knew I couldn't leave my parents. Not yet, they were too raw, from everything we'd been through as a family. I stayed at home with them for four long years.

This was my late start. The beginning of living on my own. I couldn't wait to dig in and do this.

"I've got a bottle of Pinot Gris in the fridge. You want a glass? I think we should celebrate."

I loved Pinot Gris. He knew that. Just like he knew everything about me. "Yes! That would be perfect."

He looked around my room. "When I rented this place I had you in mind. This has always been your room."

That made my eyes sting with tears. Eli wasn't one to hide his emotions. He was honest and direct about them. I loved that. But then I loved Eli. I have since we were kids. I just wasn't in love with him. There was a difference and I recognized it, at a younger age than most. Over the years I've often wondered if he understood that difference. There were moments when he looked at me with something more than friendly adoration. I'd convince myself I made it up. At least I hoped I made it up. Wanting MORE would ruin everything.

A knock on the door saved me from having to appropriately respond. Whatever that may be. I still wasn't sure how to reply to something so heartfelt. I wasn't as sensitive as Eli. What I'd been through had hardened me.

Eli turned and headed for the door. I scanned my new room one more time before I followed. Glancing over his shoulder at me he smirked. "I'd apologize about this, but I think they're being here has more to do with you than me."

"Who?"

He shook his head as he opened the door.

Micah Falco walked in carrying a six-pack followed by Damon Victor, Micah's best friend and Jude Falco, who was Micah's younger brother. Micah was twenty-five. He had a master's degree in computer science, yet he looked like a thug. Micah drank like a fish, cursed like a sailor, and was the most entertaining guy I knew, the exception being his dad, who was technically his uncle. Long story.

"Move a girl in and don't invite the fucking team. Hardy, you suck," Micah said, placing the beer on the bar. "By the way, this is mine, I'm not sharing. I assumed it was BYOB."

Damon had a case in his arms. He laid the beer right beside it. "I brought enough for me and the kid."

The kid was Jude. He was nineteen. Since he'd grown up with Micah and his friends he acted ten years older.

"Call me a fucking kid again and I'll shove those beers up your ass." He then walked past Damon with a scowl. He was four inches taller than Damon and expanding before our eyes. By twenty-five he would be huge.

"Touchy ass bastard," Damon muttered.

"You're finally free, B," Micah grinned with a beer in his hand. "How's it feel? Liberating?"

"How the hell do you think it feels? She's free of her crazy, wild ass brothers," Jude answered for me as he retrieved a beer from the counter and popped it open.

Jude was only a year older than Cruz and the two were close. That was why he could get away with bashing my brothers. He loved them like family and I knew that.

"It was hard to leave," I responded. "Difficult on mom and dad. But now I've done it, I feel great. Exactly like I thought it would."

Damon leaned against the counter and winked at me. This was his normal thing. He liked to flirt, tease and annoy. I ignored him, but of course he continued. "Now that you're free of Cage 'scary ass' York hovering over you, we can finally go on that date. Remember, you promised me one."

I rolled my eyes. I'd never promised Damon a date and I never would.

"That was in your dreams dickhead. Last night's tug and pump," Jude filthily shot back at him.

He held up his can of beer. "You're drinking my beer so your underage ass better watch what the fuck you say."

Jude didn't look worried in the least. He sat on a stool, tipped the can, emptying half its contents.

"If everyone is drinking, who's driving?" I asked realizing I sounded like my mother. Exactly like my mother.

"Walking to my parents," Micah said. He then sat on the sofa across from me. His parents lived on the beach. It was only a short distance away. "You know your dad owned one of these condos way back in the day. Dad said it was the one above this one." He told me then pointed at the ceiling.

Of course, I already knew that. Eli's parents had both lived with my dad back then. That was how they met. My dad and Eli's mom, Willow, were best friends growing up. A lot like us. Eli's dad, Marcus, had become dad's roommate and fell in love with Willow.

"Yeah, we know," Eli responded, walking to the fridge for the wine. He knew as well as I did no one was leaving anytime soon. As for myself, I was happy about that. This was what I'd missed. Living a life where friends came over and brought beer. They'd stay too late and we'd laugh and talk about things we'd never say in front of parents.

The doorbell rang. Eli looked towards it. "Who else is coming?" he asked. Eli knew that Micah knew the answer.

"I'd say that's probably Saffron and Holland or possibly Crimson and Larissa."

"My sister? Shit." Eli muttered.

Crimson was the eldest of his two younger sisters and Larissa was his aunt, though only twenty-five years old.

Saffron and Holland Corbin were twins and although there was no blood relation they were still family. We were all family. A lot of kids that had been raised together in this small town.

The door swung open before Eli could touch it. "Let the party begin! I've arrived!" Saffron announced herself as she walked in the room hoisting two cheap bottles of wine. She was nineteen and had bought them. No telling how she did that. Larissa wouldn't buy them for her.

"God help us all," Jude mumbled.

I just smiled. This was it. What I'd been missing all this time.

~NATE FINLAY~

I MADE UP an excuse to stay away from the shop and not complete Octavia's "to do" list. My excuse would run the rest of the week. To compensate for my betrayal, I unpacked her things at the new house Octavia had purchased. It was beachfront property and massive. More house than she needed, even with me visiting, because she had no friends in the area. No reason to entertain. Octavia required luxury and apparently, this was it. She wouldn't be your typical small business owner that struggled to make ends meet.

By Friday night I was ready to have a drink and relax. I had to face the shop again. While Bliss York wasn't there. I'd work Saturday and Sunday to get it done. But tonight, I was going out. There was a club in town that played live music, a place where locals went. I wasn't in the mood for the touristy shit, which was most of this town.

Octavia hadn't called to check on things. She knew I would handle anything that came up and that should make me happy. Instead, it greatly annoyed me. Didn't women normally text or call their fiancés? Wasn't that fucking normal procedure? When did I become so needy?

I grabbed the keys to my truck and headed out the door. I should fucking be thrilled she wasn't clingy. Matter of fact it was one of the things that initially attracted me to her. Suddenly that was an issue?

No it wasn't. I needed a whiskey.

The lights outside the club flashed LIVE BAY repeatedly. This was it, the rumored spot, the place I'd heard all about. I could hear the music pumping through the speakers with my truck doors shut and windows rolled up. Hell, I already liked it.

Parking was easy since the usual summer crowd was yet to arrive in masses. We needed something like this in Rosemary Beach, or we'd needed something like this. Seeing as I wasn't settling down there I don't guess it mattered now.

I remembered seeing this place as a kid. Bliss said it was popular. Some friends of her father owned LIVE BAY. The guy had once played here or something. I couldn't remember the details. They had whisky and that was my only concern.

While heading towards the entrance I tried not to think about Bliss, which meant I was thinking about her. That summer. Keeping my distance had helped, I think. Truth was, after a week of avoiding her, I wanted to just tell her the truth. Be done with the whole damn thing. That seemed like the best idea.

The only problem with that was that I was afraid I'd like what I was getting to know. What was now in front of me daily. That the woman she'd become would be twice as appealing as the girl she'd been back then. I didn't have room in my drama free life for the chaos that would create. And I wanted to keep it that way.

The band started with a cover of a Jax Stone song and I almost turned and walked out. I didn't much care for him. Even less for the music he wrote. Then again it was only one song and I needed a fucking drink.

"Hello Nate," the sweet familiarity of that voice rang in my ear, because I'd hid from the voice all week. I almost cursed when I turned to reply.

She was here. Of course, she was. She knew the owner. She'd told me all about it, but that was years ago. I knew she might be here. Deep down I'd thought about it. I couldn't pretend like I hadn't.

"Hey," I said with a smile, that I knew didn't reach my eyes. It was more forced than anything else, but I had to make some effort.

"I didn't know you were still in town," she said. "I had a question for Octavia and didn't want to bother her. Could you stop by tomorrow? It's a shipment that appears to be doubled."

She was all business. No flirting. No looking at me with those sorrowful eyes wanting me to remember. She was over it. Moved on from the shock.

"Yeah, I can. What time?"

"B! Get your ass over here! Tell this sonofabitch I can drink ten tequilas and still walk a straight line!" The male voice yelled out from a table nearby. I glanced over and saw three guys. One was Eli and a couple of women I'd never seen before. They were all laughing at the man who was demanding Bliss's confirmation of his ten-shot tequila stroll. She wouldn't help him out. She shook her head and denied his boasting.

"I'm not doing it. You'll have to prove it!"

The guy threw his hands into the air. "What the fuck, B! Damn baby, I thought you had my back!"

She rolled her eyes and looked at me. "I better get over there before Micah convinces Jimmy to do what he's saying he can do.

Because I happen to know the last time Jimmy tried it he slept it off in jail. See you tomorrow. Whenever. I'll be at the shop all day."

She didn't wait on me to respond before heading back to the table. The guys who weren't Eli looked older than her. The one threatening to drink ten shots couldn't be younger than thirty. Bliss apparently ran with a mature rough crowd, which I didn't expect from her.

One of the girls at her table had her eyes locked on me. I could feel it, but I didn't look her way. I'd caught enough of a glimpse to know she was tall, built well, and barely dressed. This told me she liked the attention. I had no time for that.

"Bring your friend with you!" the female called out, her words slurring and finishing with pauses. She was slobbering drunk and brave.

I didn't hear Bliss's response, but I watched her say something to the girl. It made her frown and turn back to the group at the table and I was left alone.

The older guy put his arm around Bliss's shoulders. She laughed loudly, closing her eyes. I hadn't seen that in years. I then realized I missed that laugh. It hadn't changed. It was the same.

Before they all saw me watching and inspecting I headed for the bar to get a drink, keeping my back turned safely away, pretending she wasn't there. I was curious to see her out with friends and wanted to know about her life. Lying to myself was pointless. She lived here. Here was familiar. Bliss had her own set of friends. I wasn't part of that and it stung. My God, I'm losing my mind.

"You know Bliss?" The bartender was an attractive female and had her large boobs barely covered by her top. She was definitely something to look at. I figured it made for good tips. I would guess she was about my age.

"She works for my fiancé," I said, although that wasn't how I saw her.

She nodded. "Good girl. One of the best. Your fiancé is lucky," she responded.

"Good to know. I'm sure Octavia sensed that before she hired her for the shop."

"Dakota! Ten shots of tequila!" The guy with Bliss yelled to her. "This thing is going down!"

The bartender sighed then spoke. "No, Jimmy it's not. The last time you tried that shit Preston had to bail you out. Before your dad got wind and killed you."

"Shiii-iit!" was his response. "I was younger. Now I'm grown. Why can't y'all just forget that?"

The bartender looked at me. "He was twenty-five when it happened. Jimmy is a hell raiser, same as his brother. What can I get you?"

"Maker's Mark," I replied, and though I didn't want to, I let myself glance back at the table. I didn't see the guy called Jimmy. I saw Bliss staring right at me. She jerked her gaze away when I caught her, but the smile that touched my lips, was as genuine as the whiskey I sipped.

Bliss York was curious.

Fucking hell.

Chapter Four

❤ BLISS YORK ❤

"**Y**OU SHOULD PROBABLY stop looking at your boss's fiancé as if you want to eat him." Saffron spoke then leaned into me, giggling and pinching my arm.

The guys shouldn't let her drink. For starters, she was underage. Following that she was a terrible drunk. Annoying to say the least. Her twin Holland wasn't with her tonight. Probably home studying or reading. They were identical in looks and height, but complete opposites in the way they lived.

"I'm not looking at him," I lied.

She cackled loudly and snorted. Did I mention she was an annoying drunk? Her dad owned the place. He was in my parents' circle of friends. Her dad was famous in a small town. Krit Corbin once played on that stage. But when he married Blythe he saved his money and bought the place outright. From then on he stayed off the road. The road wasn't for married people. At least that was what dad had said.

If he walked in the door and saw Saffron drunk, there would be hell to pay. She stayed in trouble. So, the guys all watched her and kept her from doing anything additionally stupid. More so than she'd already done. I knew she wouldn't make it five short steps in Nate's direction before Eli blocked her. Micah would then carry her out on his shoulder like he was toting a sack of feed.

"I'm sorry Bliss, you're ogling his ass. Is that a more accurate description?"

I had been looking at him. Acting like I wasn't, was pointless. Besides, Saffron was obliviously drunk and wouldn't remember this. I didn't think she'd remember this. Saffron, PLEASE don't remember this.

"Eli, let's dance," I said. I wasn't having this conversation with 'Saffron the drunk' anymore. Though she wouldn't give it a break. "Yeah! Eli go dance with her! Then she'll stop staring at Mr. Sexy As Hell guy over there at the bar!" I winced as she yelled her words just as the music died down.

"Someone needs to cut her off." I didn't mumble. She didn't care.

"Already have," Micah assured me. "Dakota has been serving her straight club soda for the past hour and a half. Larissa isn't working tonight but Dakota knows the rules when it comes to Saffron."

Saffron frowned. "That's not fair. I know you're discussing me."

"Life's a bitch sweetheart," Micah replied, which made Jimmy burst into laughter. Someone needed to serve him club soda. I didn't care if he'd turn thirty on his birthday. It was past time Jimmy found a woman and settled into a pattern. Calmed down, stop living in bars. His older brother Brent had straightened up after marrying Chloe. Jimmy had no interest in that. Didn't seem to be heading in that direction.

Eli was looking back at the bar toward Nate as he walked over to me. His forehead was drawn with concern. He still hadn't met the adult Nate. He hadn't seen him since that summer. It had been long enough for Nate to forget so I figured Eli had to.

I hoped Eli had forgotten. I knew the others hadn't seen Nate but from a distance that summer. Micah was the only one other than Eli and Larissa that got a good look at the sixteen-year-old boy he had been. He was a man now and although I recognized him I felt fairly sure they wouldn't.

"Who is that?" Eli asked.

He would remember. I knew him well enough to know Eli hadn't forgotten.

"The fiancé of my boss."

"Why does he look familiar?"

And there it was. Eli's excellent memory.

"Because it's Nate Finlay," I admitted. I then waited for Eli's response.

He paused and studied me a moment. When his eyes widened, they were big. "The guy from that summer," he whispered, before looking back at Nate. "He's Octavia's fiancé?"

"Yes." Now he was going to ask me why I didn't tell him this at the store. I counted to ten in my head and I knew what was coming next.

"Why didn't you tell me who he was?"

I shrugged. "He didn't remember. I didn't want him to hear me. You know I need that job."

Again he looked back at Nate. "He remembers."

I started to argue the point when Eli slipped his hand through mine. "Let's go dance," he said.

I wanted to ask him how he knew Nate remembered. To go beyond what he'd already said but I needed to let it go. Besides, I was doing my best to pretend that Nate wasn't Nate. Not the Nate that I knew, just some other guy who happened to be known by that name, and was marrying the woman I worked for. That was all I knew how to do.

We danced two songs before Micah cut in and then I danced a few times with him. Eli came back and interrupted us. We needed to get Saffron home.

"Can't take her home like that. Blythe will fucking shit." Micah spoke and he was right. Her mother would not be happy. But then again, Saffron, who was a lunatic, rarely did something to please them.

"She can stay with me," I told him.

Eli scoffed. "Not sure that's a good idea. I don't want Krit Corbin on my ass. If he finds out she's drunk and being hidden . . ."

"Jimmy should take her. She's his cousin," Micah interrupted.

Seriously? When was Jimmy ever responsible for anyone but himself? "That's a terrible idea," I responded. "Might as well throw her in a ditch."

Eli nodded in agreement. "Can we call Holland for help?" Poor Holland had to bail her twin out of trouble on an average of once a week. I hated to do this to her, but there wasn't any other choice.

"Yeah, I'll call her," I said.

Both guys seemed happy about that. I left them to head back to the table where my phone was tucked away in my purse. I tried really hard not to look at Nate as I swerved across the floor. I finally compromised and let my gaze slide past where he was sitting, but he was gone. Although I felt disappointed, which was silly, I knew it was for the best. I didn't need any more temptation.

I could've invited Nate to our table so he wouldn't have been alone. But then everyone would talk and he could remember and my embarrassment would know no bounds. That he had forgotten me, forgotten our summer, was a thing I preferred to keep to myself.

"Your boy left!" Saffron yelled, before I was even close to the table.

I ignored her. What else could I do?

"He sauntered out of here looking like sex on a motherfuckin' stick," she added.

"Why is she calling him your boy? You didn't tell her about that summer did you?"

I snapped back at Eli quickly. "Of course not. She wanted to go hit on him and so she asked me who he was. I said he was my boss's fiancé and that the man was very taken."

Eli nodded but didn't look thrilled. I'd moved out of my parent's house. I didn't need Eli hovering, and worrying like they do. Surely, he knew that.

"Eli, stop it with the concerned frown. That was a long time ago. I've all but forgotten it. Besides for once in my life I want to be treated like I'm grown up and independent. Can you please let me?"

"Yeah, I know, B.C." he said.

B.C. meant before cancer. It was the way we labeled my sickness. B.C., D.C. and A.C. Before, during and after.

"Exactly," I responded. We both knew everything B.C. was from a different life and era. One where we didn't know fear or pain, or if we did it was temporary. My cancer had ignited our perfect worlds and shown us that life was fragile.

~NATE FINLAY~

I WAS HERE like I promised. I just hadn't got out of my truck yet. I was giving myself a pep talk. Which was ridiculous considering our history. She was nothing but a childhood fling. One that I was pretending I didn't remember, which explained me sitting in my vehicle.

"This is a higher level of coward," I said to myself out loud.

Shaking my head with disgust I got out and headed for the door. The backdoor. Not the front. Bliss had a question about a shipment. I would answer then be on my way. The list that I had of "to do's" at the place was a half mile long or better, but I couldn't stay in there with Bliss. Alone, where I could see her and smell her.

Octavia wasn't going to be happy if she got back and her shit wasn't finished. I should stay today and get things done. Stop being a dick and hiding. She hadn't said anything about that summer. Maybe she'd forgotten me too? Lies. I'm lying to myself. Like me, Bliss remembered. I'd seen it on her face the moment we locked eyes. It was as if we were still there. Younger, happier and knowing. Knowing we'd never forget this.

Opening the backdoor I walked inside and stopped short when I saw Bliss's ass. Stuck up into the air being asslike. It was a nice one. No, scratch that. It was a stellar one and I thoroughly enjoyed the view. The shorts she was wearing rode up high and perfectly cupped her stellar ass. Damn.

She then began to shake that ass, as she remained bent at the waist. She must have heard me come in. Was that why she'd asked me to meet her here? To shake her ass at me? That wasn't a horrible plan. Currently it was working for her.

"Shake it off, shake it off!" she sang rather loudly, and on key I might add. She then straightened and shook it some more. This time her hips joined in and she did this thing with her hands. It was cute. Blended well with her hips. Bliss York was dancing and I was almost positive she had no idea there was an audience.

She began singing another line, interpreting moves as she unpacked the box. The polite thing to do would be to let her know I was here "not" enjoying myself. Which would be another fucking lie. My guess was she had in ear buds, and couldn't hear a thing but the music. I wasn't polite. I let the door close behind me with a thud. That didn't make her jump so I leaned against the wall crossing my arms to watch. Eventually she'd spin around and here I would be. Bliss would become embarrassed. A nice guy would feel bad about that. As for myself I owed her one. She'd crushed my young heart seven years ago. I might as well make her blush and cringe. Besides, she was giving me a very fond memory, one I would never forget.

The "shake it off" song must've ended. Suddenly she belted out "baby, this is what you came for!" I recognized that song. I was impressed with her Rihanna rendition.

Though she didn't get very far into the song. It was then she threw up her hands, turning in a circle that became a squeal when she saw me standing there. I didn't move. I just grinned. Then slowly clapped my hands.

She jerked the white cord of her ear buds. As expected her face turned bright red and I felt a little guilty for that. But damn, this was fun to watch. I could get over being a dick. I liked seeing Bliss this way.

For a moment, she was the girl I remembered. The one that made that summer. Now the woman, the Bliss of now, the thing she'd grown into, stammered for something to say.

"I was hoping you'd get to the good part. I think you'd do it better than her. Definitely give her a run for her money."

I was trying to tease so she'd laugh. It worked, she pressed her lips together, and released a loud giggle. "How long were you standing there?"

"Long enough to see your repertoire of ass wiggling, hip jerking and impressive shimmies I had no idea existed."

Again, she laughed and covered her face with both hands hiding her embarrassment. "Oh God!"

"I was entertained as hell."

She shook her head. I waited until she finally dropped her hands and smiled Bliss York's huge grin. It was like a punch in the gut. As if time hadn't happened and she was still fifteen, the smile the same, genuine, full of life. Back then that's what I loved the most, Bliss enjoying everything. She found the good in everyone without any jealousy or any of the negative shit I was accustomed to hearing from girls my age. She didn't do that, had no interest in anger or spite.

I once thought her smile the most beautiful thing I'd ever seen because she meant it. Nothing fake in its delivery or meaning. Seeing it again I knew it was the same, no matter what happened after that summer, she was still Bliss York. Now she was just older, more mature and more beautiful.

"I didn't expect you until later." She appeared to be explaining herself.

"Clearly," I agreed.

She let out a sigh and another small giggle. Bliss nodded her chin to the left. Towards the boxes stacked on the side. "I need to know what to do with those. Three boxes, the exact same order. I know Octavia loves the Jimmy Choo scarves. The ones she found in Italy were shipped here then these others arrived. I don't think she wanted that many in stock. She means to keep smaller quantities, to make them more exclusive, and these seem to be overkill. I believe there's been a mistake."

The way Bliss spoke with so much knowledge of Octavia's vision for the store impressed the hell out of me. They'd only met once in the interview. Bliss paid attention and remembered. Octavia had been smart in hiring her.

"I agree. She wouldn't order that many. It's about to be hot as hell for the next few months. Few people will be buying scarves."

Bliss nodded. "That's what I was thinking. Could she have ordered for her father's stores?"

That was a possibility. I could call her and ask but this was something Bliss had caught for Octavia. And Octavia needed to know that. My fiancé wasn't easy to impress and she was hard where Bliss was soft. I wanted Bliss to do well and succeed. Nothing had been handed to her, whereas Octavia, well, had been given the moon and then asked if she'd like condos on its surface. I admit the same goes for me, but I'd learned to appreciate drive, in those who had to make it by themselves.

"Call her, tell her and see what she says."

Bliss frowned. "You want me to call?"

She sounded terrified, which was good. Octavia could be a mean bitch. Bliss just had to impress her.

"Yeah, Octavia hired you, she needs to hear it from you."

Bliss chewed on her bottom lip and I wanted to chew on it to. Jerking my gaze off her mouth I silently cursed myself.

"When?"

"Now."

"Now now?"

"Yep, right this second."

She inhaled deeply, squared her shoulders and simply replied "okay." That one word sounded like she was going into battle. It was fucking adorable.

"Thank you for stopping by."

I shrugged. "I was coming in anyway. I've got a shit ton of things to work on. I'll be here most of the day."

She looked as surprised as me.

Chapter Fire

♥ BLISS YORK ♥

OCTAVIA WAS FURIOUS about the order. She had me get the invoice, read it entirely and when I gave her the balance she freaked, cursing a blue streak and threatening the lives of those who were to blame. I had to admit her anger was justified. Paying thirty thousand dollars for scarves she didn't order would make me have a stroke. She'd ordered ten, receiving sixty. I was instructed to repack them, though I hadn't unpacked them, only had a peek. Then return them all. The supplier had made a mistake. She wouldn't be buying any scarves from them. I thought that was a bit overboard. She was carrying Jimmy Choo items and it was an honest mistake but I didn't say so.

Once that was all handled the new shipment arrived. Light shoes, swimsuits, summer wear in general, the things she wanted displayed. Octavia wouldn't buy more than ten of each item and those sizes were select and popular. If anyone wore something larger than an eight they shouldn't step foot inside this place. She carried double zeros, up to size eight, and only one size eight per item.

I thought it was a little elitist and exclusive, which was exactly what Octavia was. This was an elitist and exclusive store. The more I got to know Octavia through her calls, along with the texts she sent, I realized she thought that way. I myself didn't exclude anyone, because I didn't want to be excluded. This, of course, made me wonder about Nate. Who had he become? Someone attracted to that?

I didn't want to judge him. I knew nothing about their relationship and it was unfair to make assumptions. But I did once know Nate. He was nothing at all like Octavia. He came from privilege and wealth, however, he didn't act entitled. Currently he was standing on a ladder in the shop putting fancy light bulbs in the chandelier Octavia had him hang.

He hadn't said much after telling me to call her. Well, actually, Nate hadn't spoken at all. He'd stayed up front while I worked in the back. We had a moment this morning laughing at my dancing, when I saw that gleam in his eyes. I thought for a second he remembered me. Us. But then he said nothing at all.

I tried not to let that defeat me. I also tried not allowing resurfacing memories to make me sad, spiteful and angry. There'd been a connection, that connection was gone, I would never experience it again. My experience with men was limited. I thought that was mostly the problem.

"You ready for lunch?" Nate asked. His voice startled me, I flinched, jerking up my head from the bikinis I was displaying.

"What?" I stammered. "Huh?"

He smirked and it was ridiculously attractive. "Do you eat?"

I nodded. What kind of question was that?

"Then are you ready to eat some lunch?"

Oh. He was asking about my lunch break. I rarely took one unless Eli stopped by and Eli wasn't here. "I guess. I usually don't stop unless Eli comes and stops me."

Nate pulled his keys from his pocket. "That's not healthy.

You should eat. Let's go. I know a place."

I stood up and stared at him. The keys jingled in his hand. He wanted to take me to lunch? Would Octavia be okay with that?

"Oh, um." I didn't know what to say. Although the idea of eating lunch with him and riding in his truck were tempting.

"Stop over thinking it Bliss. Let's go eat. We've earned a lunch."

I managed a nod and walked over to my purse. This was normal. We worked together. In a way he was my boss. He wanted to take me to lunch.

"Okay."

"I see you've not unpacked the boxes. She must've said to send them back."

"Yeah. She wasn't happy."

He chuckled. "I bet she wasn't."

There it was. The way he chuckled like he knew her and she amused him. Its warmth, the way he delivered it, the jealousy bit me hard. I hadn't ever dealt with that before, but now it was here and it was hard. It sucked. What a horrible feeling. The top of my head went numb.

"How long have y'all been together?" I tried to act like it didn't bother me.

Nate locked up the back and we headed to his truck.

"Since our freshman year of college."

College. Something else I missed. Actually going to a campus. I'd taken all my classes online and in the fall would complete my courses. Then my student teaching. I hoped the school where I taught would hire me. Elementary education wasn't in high demand. Not around here it wasn't. There were too many teachers wanting to teach on the coast. Maybe I could go inland? Perhaps to a poorer county? That's where teachers were needed most.

"Did you go to college?" he asked. I hated having to answer

this. Unless he knew my past and all about the cancer it looked like I'd taken a short cut. Gone for the easy way out. I could explain it, but then, like every other man, he would immediately treat me different. Like I was fragile and consumed with disease. I didn't want to be the sick girl. I wanted to be normal and this was my chance to finally live like my friends. And if he didn't remember me, or acknowledge that summer, I would view that as part of the cycle of living a normal life. Though currently it was aggravating.

"Yes," I replied. That's all. I then asked "where are we eating?" The subject had to be changed.

"My grandpop's place. Best shrimp poboys in town."

I'd eaten there seven years ago. In fact, numerous times. Would his grandpop remember me? I never went back after that summer. It was an off-limits place for me. I hadn't wanted to go in without my hair and have his grandpop report to Nate, which he probably wouldn't have done. But my need to preserve our summer and the memory of it had been too important. Every time I passed his place I remembered Nate. I thought about him and wondered if he came to visit his grandfather often. Now I knew.

I wasn't sure what I should say. If I asked him questions about it then it was like I was lying. I already knew the answers. So, I stayed quiet. He could talk if he wanted.

"Last night at the club, were those your friends?" Thank you Jesus, he was changing the subject.

"For the most part, yes, they were. Some forced upon me since birth. Our parents are all very close. We grew up like family."

"The drunk girl," he began and I laughed.

"Saffron. Her dad owns the place. She's a train wreck most of the time."

"She asked me to dance. That's why I left. When I said no as nicely as I could she began to rub my thigh. I like hot women rubbing my thigh, but she was highly intoxicated, and I'm guessing underage."

I winced. I'd missed that. "She's nineteen. And stays in trouble. My daddy says that her dad is getting paid back for the hell he raised when he was younger."

Nate laughed. "Mom used to say the same about me. That I was my dad's payback."

The Nate I knew hadn't been a hell raiser. Those were years I didn't know.

~NATE FINLAY~

I KNEW GRANDPOP would recognize her. But I was going to take her there anyway. This was impulsive. Possibly stupid. A desire to do something we'd once done that would make her remember me. What we were doing was once our thing. But why did I have to do it? I was the one playing dumb. I knew who was sitting beside me. What she was and what she'd meant. I also didn't have to remind her. She hadn't forgotten.

I pulled into the parking lot. Grandpop's blue 1989 Chevy was parked in the back as usual. I loved that truck. Its sight was comforting, the Chevy seemingly permanent, because the man was always here. And he could force me to admit the past. Unless, I got to him first and asked him not to say a word.

He'd think I was crazy and probably blurt it out. Grandpop hated Octavia. Said she was trouble and a "sure fire divorce". He'd already been divorced twice. The woman he spent his life with now was a widow and they both agreed marriage was not for them.

"Ever been here?" I asked Bliss, knowing full well she had been. I just wanted to see if she'd be honest.

She stared at the place for a few long seconds before turning her gaze to me. "Yes," she simply replied. But with that response her eyes lit up and I felt like a dick again. But of course, if I admitted it now, then everything would become difficult.

"Then you know how good the food is." I should have said more than that. But I didn't. It was best for the both of us that I keep it this way.

She nodded, but said nothing more.

I had to get out of this truck. Put some distance between our bodies. Preferably where I couldn't smell her. Or reach over and touch her. I loved Octavia in a way of speaking. Loved the idea of "us." We fit. The sex was hot. She wasn't needy. It was and had been the easiest relationship I'd ever had. I'd be stupid to destroy it.

Opening my door, I got out. Inhaling the sea breeze deeply cleared my nose of Bliss's sweet scent. I listened as she opened her door. My mother would be ashamed of me for not running around to do that. Octavia demanded that kind of thing, though Octavia didn't really deserve it. On the other hand, well, Bliss did. Octavia would've waited until I came for her door, then emerged like she owned the place.

Bliss was waiting for me to stop staring at the water. I had to get my head together. Whether grandpop would agree to play along wasn't easy to predict or know. Before he saw her, I would intervene. Debrief him, shit like that.

"Let's go eat." I shot her a friendly smile and started for the door of the restaurant. She fell into step beside me.

"Does your grandpop work here?" she asked. I glanced. She was looking at his truck. He'd had that truck since he moved here. Bliss had seen it before. She knew it was his and was wondering if he'd remember her.

"Yep. Never missed a day."

She gave me a tight, nervous smile. I opened the door then stood back and let Bliss go inside first. At least my momma would be happy about that. Even if she wouldn't approve of everything else I'd done concerning Bliss and all my secrecy. Along with not opening the truck door.

When I stepped in I saw grandpop animatedly speaking to the bartender. He'd always been happy here. That made my mother happy. Once he was dark and depressed. Grandpop made some bad mistakes but my mom forgave him. Because his mistakes had led her to my dad. That was a mushy, fairytale story I'd heard too many times. They took being in love way *too far* for the reality of the world around them. I'd never go in like that. Too deep. Too fucking deep. People didn't stay together anymore. I wasn't going to get myself burned. Octavia couldn't burn me. She was safe. The effort was minimal.

"Pick a table. I'll be right there." I then beelined for my grandpop. He noticed me headed his way, a smile spreading across his face.

"Look who can't stay away from his grandpop's cooking."

"Nothing beats you," I assured him. He liked being told that even if it wasn't the actual truth of the matter. This place was more of a bar, though the food was above average for the bar cuisine and takeout. His poboys really were good.

He stepped from behind the bar. Opened his arms to hug me. "Haven't seen you in a couple of days. How've you been eating?"

"I grab something here and there. Been working on Octavia's shit."

He frowned at her name. Grandpop didn't approve. Then his eyes fell on Bliss and he paused. I gave him the moment he needed.

"I'll be damned, that one made a beauty. Glad you looked her up. Remind yourself what a good woman is."

"I didn't. She works for Octavia. I haven't told her I remember her. She thinks I've forgotten that summer and her and I'd like to keep it that way. She's a good employee and Octavia needs someone, so please don't make it complicated."

Grandpop didn't respond. His expression told me enough. He'd thought I'd lost my marbles. "Are you shitting me right now?"

I shook my head.

"Well, hell."

"It's just easier if our past stays there."

"Easier than what? Truth?" He sighed. "I'll keep my mouth shut, but not for you, and your fancy ass fiancé. I'll do it for that girl over there. She was sweet. Doesn't need to get hurt. They raised money for her back when she was sick. I donated poboys to the community event. Even with insurance, which will tend to fuck you over, her hospital bills were steep. I have no idea how her parents got the hell out from under them. It's all a goddamned roll of the dice."

Sick? What? What bills? "I don't know what you're talking about."

"The girl beat cancer. Fought and won the war. Strong girl. Town really loves her."

"Cancer?" What the fuck did he mean she had cancer?

He nodded. "Yeah. She's got a lot of friends in Sea Breeze. Worried the whole bunch to death."

I looked back at Bliss. Letting his words sink in. Never had I imagined she'd lived through something like that. She was more mature, older, less naïve but I thought that all came with age. Not a brush with death. She didn't look our way. She was intensely studying a menu.

"When did she get sick? Why didn't you tell me?"

"Happened after that summer. The one you spent with her. I figured you knew. Didn't want to upset you by talking about the inevitable. I was going to let you bring it up if you wanted to further discuss it. You were just a kid then. I hated for you to see the ugly this world has so soon."

Bliss looked up from her menu. She smiled and I saw a flash of sorrow in her eyes and across her brow. I'd missed it before, but there it was, hope, sorrow and something else. It was joy. Bliss was happy. Not because she hadn't known struggle or fear, but because she'd faced them head on, and won. Shit, I was sinking in deep.

Chapter Six

♥ BLISS YORK ♥

I READ THE menu through three times before Nate came back to the table. By then it was memorized. I could feel him looking at me. It made me nervous in a way that was both good and bad and then it all ran together. I wondered if his grandfather was reminding him about me. If he did would it change in an instant? Would my employment with Octavia end?

When Nate sat down beside me my nerves were shot from the stress and the pressure of what would come from their talk at the bar. I couldn't look up from my memorized menu until Nate put me at ease.

"Find anything you want?" he casually asked. There was nothing in his voice to warn me that he knew or didn't know. He seemed the same. Maybe his grandfather had forgotten who I was and what had happened. Had they simply been discussing that Octavia had hired me and the lunch was a professional courtesy?

"I think I'm going to trust you and go with the shrimp poboy." When I told him I smiled then brought the grin up to look into his eyes with confidence.

He nodded. "Good choice. Smart move."

I felt my smile wobble and took a quick peek at his grandfather who was watching intently. Was he seeing how I reacted to his stare? Did he know that I knew he knew that I knew . . . ugh, I was losing my mind. In my head, I recited the list of appetizers without looking at the menu. Then I checked to make sure I got them right. Not a miss. Was I going insane?

"I can't believe you don't come here regularly. The place is pretty popular." Was he testing me now? Fishing for clues? Jesus, the pressure of this lunch.

"I don't eat out much." I wasn't going to lie.

He didn't appear surprised or confused by my response. He appeared his normal relaxed self. "So when was the last time you were here?"

I gave a small shrug with my shoulders. "It's been years. It looks the same." Just saying the words was tough. Knowing he didn't hold those memories as close to his heart as me. Or at all.

There must have been oodles of girls since me. I blended in with all those women. I was just another name in a journal. I winced. I hoped he didn't have a journal of women.

"Hasn't changed much I'd guess. What was your favorite dish when you came in here before?"

To have a favorite I would've had to try several things. He was assuming I had been more than once. Or was I reading too much into this?

"I never came enough to have a favorite."

He smirked then shifted his eyes to the bar where I knew his grandfather was studying. Maybe he'd clued Nate in with a little memory jolt?

"You're right. I assumed that once you'd eaten here you'd want to come back repeatedly. My mistake. Forgive me. Sorry."

My heart sank a little. That was it. All he was going to say. Every time I was faced with Nate forgetting me it hurt. I wished

it didn't, but the pain was overwhelming. If I'd had more experience with guys it probably wouldn't sting as bad. The few I'd
dated hadn't been anything memorable. They weren't enough
compared to Nate. They never clicked, because they couldn't
be him, which was my own personal dilemma. I just wished he
thought the same about me.

Now it seemed like those guys, though few in number, may
have been a good thing nevertheless. This entire time I'd been
fixated on a fantasy that obviously wasn't meant to be. I wasn't
important enough to remember.

"Octavia won't eat here. It's below her. Grandpop says that
I should take note. A girl who will walk through those doors is a
keeper, according to the old man over there."

I didn't respond to that. It wasn't my business, although I did
agree, you had to accept one's family. This was his grandfather's
restaurant. Octavia should want to come here. But then of course
I'd met Octavia. She wasn't the type to be considerate of others
unless it benefitted her. She did what she wanted to do.

"When will Octavia be back? She didn't say anything on the
phone."

Nate shrugged. "Hell if I know. She comes and goes on a
whim. You'll see soon enough."

That didn't sound like a healthy relationship. Was that what
Nate desired? Wanted to be married to forever? A wealthy socialite that lived a life of leisure and ran a business as entertainment?
No, that wasn't fair. Octavia was working hard to make this a
successful business. Sure her father was there if she needed him
with unlimited money but she wasn't to blame for that.

"In high school where did you and your friends hang out?"

Nate's question came from out of the blue. I didn't want to
answer it. My life in high school wasn't what he thought. Telling
the truth would give away too much. Yet I wasn't going to lie, so

I chose a vague reply. "Here and there. Not too much to choose from around here if you want to stay away from the tourist."

He chuckled. "Here and there? Really? That's all I get?"

I shrugged and turned the question on him. "Where did you and your friends hang out?"

"The Kerrington Country Club. The beach and clubs in Destin." He then paused and finished with a wink. "That's the way you answer a question."

I sighed. He was right.

"I didn't go out a lot. I stayed home mostly. Eli was my only close friend."

There, that was the truth. All he was getting from me.

"Why?" He frowned, but it wasn't a frown of confusion, he was pressing me for more information. He was curious. I'd have to answer.

"Because I was an introvert. I liked my house and the safety there. I wasn't good with people and Eli understood me. It worked because it had to. There was no other choice for me."

"You don't seem introverted."

He didn't know the girl who'd fought cancer. He knew the survivor. The outcome. My before and during cancer were something else entirely. "People change. Circumstances change you."

His grandfather appeared at the table with two beers and sat them down. "Y'all decided on something to eat?"

I hated beer. But I kept my mouth shut. I could sip it to wash down my food.

"Two shrimp poboys with the chips you make. Extra salt. My blood pressure's low."

His grandfather nodded then smiled at me when I met his gaze with mine. "Good to have you back," he said. Then he walked away.

I became a block of ice. Unsure if I should look at Nate.

"You must've made an impression on grandpop when you

did come in before." He leaned back and took a drink of his beer. "Do you even drink beer?" he asked.

I shook my head. He waved over a waitress. "Joyce, can Bliss have a . . ." he looked at me for an answer to his question.

"Sweet tea," I replied. "Thank you."

Joyce nodded. "Sure thing," then she walked away, switching her hips for Nate.

"The old man thinks the world drinks beer." He muttered, actually he whispered it. Then he added in a normal tone "did you have a favorite subject? In high school or anything after?"

The questions went on like that. Each query made me think harder about how I answered his questions. Keeping my secret was difficult, but somehow I managed it.

~NATE FINLAY~

IT WAS ALL I could think about Sunday. That damn lunch. All the answers she avoided. Asking her had been unfair. She obviously was trying her hardest to keep it a secret from me. Along with who she was. That was my fault. She thought I didn't remember and after spending time with her I realized her not reminding me was for my own benefit. Not hers.

The Bliss I'd fallen for that summer was the same. She was tougher now and had seen how ugly life can get. The girl became a woman, facing fear and winning, but her heart hadn't changed. There was a kindness inside her that you couldn't manufacture. It made you question your relationships. Had they been Bliss would it have worked?

Why the hell am I focused on this? That was a recipe for disaster. I had a good thing. The easy drama free kind of relationship all men look for. I wasn't going to mess that up with

Bliss. Even if she made me feel something I hadn't in a long time. Seeing her smile reminded me there were women out there that weren't solely concerned with their needs and simply pleasing their selfish desires.

I didn't want to ever be as vulnerable as my father. Although my momma would never hurt my father . . . what if, I mean, if he lost her. If she died he wouldn't live. He'd follow my mother in death. Sure he loved his children and had a good life, but mom was his number one. His center. A fucking necessity. That shit was scary as hell.

Octavia would never be my center. I was safe from that kind of heartbreak. I could continue on breathing and living if something happened to her. Sure I'd be sad, but I wouldn't die from it, which was healthy and normal. That was all I wanted in life. Shallow? Yes. But shallow is safe. I'd convinced myself of that.

I was jerked from my thoughts when someone bumped me and dropped a box at my feet. Books went everywhere. "Sorry man, I didn't see you. My bad. Wasn't paying attention." It was Eli. Standing in front of me.

His eyes locked on me and he straightened. There was recognition there and he wasn't hiding it like Bliss. Had she talked to him about me? Did he think I remembered what she thought I'd forgotten? My God, this was confusing.

"Please tell me you don't have a place here," were the words that came from his mouth. If it had been anyone else I'd have considered that to be rude. But I understood and respected his concern. Bliss meant a lot to him. I wondered if she meant more than that? I couldn't imagine them just being friends. I thought that would be fucking impossible. But then, of course, that was me. Eli may be different.

"My grandfather does," I replied. Not that grandpop ever stayed here. He was always at the bar. I'd told him I would come by this afternoon and eat Sunday lunch with him. It was the only day of the week that he spent his afternoon at home. The bar was closed until six in the evening on Sundays. It was kind of his day off.

"Great," Eli muttered, bending down to collect the books. I could've kept walking and left it at that, but I wanted more information. About what? Bliss, that's what. I wasn't going to act on my feelings. But I wasn't strong enough to stay away either. What I didn't know about her past was a gap I had to close.

In the end the more I knew would only cause pain when she left. I was asking for it. Normally I ignored the dramatic. This time I apparently invited it. My desire to know Bliss was now winning out over my own self-preservation.

"Pride and Prejudice, Wuthering Heights, Jane Eyre . . . interesting reading choices." I was being an ass. These were Bliss's books. She loved to read and *Pride and Prejudice* I knew was her all time favorite. I hoped the fucker hadn't scratched them up being a clumsy son of a bitch.

"Can't beat a good romance," he replied with a sarcastic drawl. He wasn't going to admit they were Bliss's. Why? Because he didn't know that I was aware they lived together as friends? He was protecting her from me. Smart man.

"Can't say I prefer that genre, but to each his own."

Eli then jammed *Sense and Sensibility* into the box with unnecessary force before standing up and glaring at me. "Not everyone knows a good thing when it slaps them in the face."

He started to walk off and I should have let him, no point in digging any deeper. He didn't like me. Probably hated me. Was Bliss talking badly about me? If so, then that sucked ass. Because other than "forgetting" her I was being nice. I thought she enjoyed her time with me yesterday at my grandpop's.

"How long has she been cancer free?" The words came out before I could stop them.

He froze. We stood there like that for what seemed to be longer than it actually was. My head was pounding with the realization I'd just admitted I knew her. Had known her. Shit. He was gonna tell her. I'd have to face the past now.

When he finally turned around to face me there was hardness in his expression. Eli seemed easy going. Kind and gentle, the sort she belonged with. He was the guy that believed in fairytales and could probably make them come true.

"You know," was all he said.

I nodded.

"Fuck you," was the response I deserved. He then walked off towards the stairs.

I stood there and waited just in case he decided to come back for answers. After five minutes I knew he wasn't returning so I walked to grandpop's condo. It was on the bottom floor.

Eli would immediately tell her. She'd know when I saw her at work. My pretending would be over and we would have to deal with it. A large portion of me was relieved.

But there was a small part of me that was terrified. Of what we would say and how things would be with us now. How strong was I? I'd soon find out.

I knocked once and the door to my grandfather's condo swung open and hit the wall. The smell of gumbo met my nose. My grandfather stood there with a black apron on that said "KISS THE COOK" in white lettering. There were tiny white handprints on it that belonged to a much younger me. My sisters handprints were on there also. My mother had us make it for him fifteen Christmases ago.

"About time you got here. I was getting close to eating this without you. There's beers in the fridge." He then returned to his kitchen.

I closed the door behind me. My thoughts drifted to the way

it looked. Was Bliss's place like this one? Was her bedroom to the left of the living room like grandpop's guest room was? Or had Eli given her the master? Or were they sleeping together in his bed?

Fuck that train of thought. It didn't sit well at all. I headed for the fridge for the first of what would more than likely be too many beers.

Chapter Seven

♥ BLISS YORK ♥

ALL AFTERNOON ELI had acted weird. Like he was nervous or anxious or jumpy. By the time we needed to leave for Jilly's third birthday party he'd barely said five words. We had to go to his grandparent's house. I wasn't looking forward to the trip. I wanted to ask him what was wrong. But asking would make us late and he didn't need to be late.

Jilly was Eli's cousin. Jilly was the youngest in their group. It was fun having a little one around. Once I thought they'd never stop coming. Then as time went on we all grew up and our parents stopped reproducing.

Larissa's pregnancy had been exciting even after the father ran off. We all supported and assisted, came together as a group and the child was well loved in his absence.

"What did you get her?" I asked. I was trying to make him talk, although I doubted I would be successful.

"Spiderman water gun."

That sounded odd for a three-year old girl. But not for Jilly, she would love it. She was a huge Spiderman fan. The birthday party invitations were Spiderman themed and I expected the party would be.

"You?" he asked.

"An art set."

"She'll love that."

"I thought so too when I bought it last week."

We headed for the door with our presents in hand. I decided to ask him what was wrong. I'd make sure we weren't late. But I couldn't go all evening without knowing why Eli was upset. Something was bothering him.

"Spill," I demanded, placing my hand on the door, to keep him from walking outside.

He tried to frown in confusion, arching his brows, like he didn't know what I meant. He failed but tried anyway. "What? Spill what? I'm confused."

I rolled my eyes. He sucked at this. "You know what. You're upset about something or there's a contract on your life by a drug cartel or the mob. I seriously doubt it's the last one. You don't even take painkillers. I wouldn't think you're into the blow."

He sighed and looked at me. His expression said "I don't want to tell" but he would or I'd become angry.

"Nate's grandfather lives in the building."

That was it? He was upset over that? Eli could be as dramatic as a female at times, so I responded "and . . . uh . . . so what?"

He shrugged. "I just don't want you running into him more often than you should."

There he was, worrying again. Like he always had and would. "Eli, I told you, I'm a big girl. Stop it with the hovering and concern. I am fine with Nate. I see him at work. I'm employed by his fiancé."

Eli didn't look convinced. Definitely not relieved. I opened the door before I lost my temper and fussed at him some more. He was way too overprotective. It was a waste of my breath I decided.

We stepped out of the condo and headed for the stairs. I wanted to say more, but I kept my mouth shut, because changing the subject was better. "Did you bring a swimsuit?" I asked him. Mine was under my sundress. Eli's grandparents had a beautiful pool on the beach and this was a swimming party.

He nodded. "Yeah."

He was still being moody. Seriously?

"Eli, what is your deal? I should be the one acting pissy. You're just being ridiculous."

We'd just gotten to the bottom of the stairs when Nate came into view. He was walking toward the parking lot. I paused and his gaze found us both. He went from Eli to me then stopped. Like he was waiting on something to happen.

"We're going to be late," Eli said, taking my arm and moving forward.

"No, we aren't." I argued.

"We are if you stop and talk."

"I was only going to be polite."

"He doesn't need polite. Doesn't fucking deserve it."

I jerked my arm loose from Eli. "What is your problem? Are you mad at him because he doesn't remember me? Eli, let that go. It was a long time back. I was a kid. I've changed. So has he."

I turned my attention back to Nate. He was watching us like a hawk. Like he expected something to explode. I got the feeling there was more to this than I realized was currently happening. Had they talked today? Had words? Did Eli say something he shouldn't?

"What's going on?" I asked Eli in a whisper. Yes, something had occurred.

He glared at Nate. "Nothing. Not a thing."

"Eli," I warned, "something's going on." He knew I'd discover the truth. No reason to hide it now.

"Why don't you ask *him?*" His tone was full of anger as he continued glaring. Eli then walked off, leaving me there with Nate. I watched as he stalked towards the car, completely baffled at his behavior.

Turning my attention back to Nate I asked "what the heck happened?"

Nate looked as confused as me. "Not sure. He was really upset."

Great, Eli was crazed over nothing and there'd been no reason for this. Nate would know if there was.

"I'm sorry. He's been acting weird all day. I'm trying to figure out what's bothering him."

Nate nodded as if he understood.

"Well, I'll see you tomorrow then." I said it and started for the car.

"Bliss." His voice stopped me.

"Yes?"

He stared at me for a moment. It made me nervous, I wanted to fix my hair or check and see if there was something in my teeth. Those silver eyes made me a mess. They always had and always would.

"When did you beat cancer?"

I felt myself break. My heart plummeted. Right there lost in his eyes. He knew. I wasn't a stranger. I was a healthy female that worked for his fiancé. Not the girl he once knew. I was A.C., no longer B.C. And they were different. Vastly different.

He'd never look at me the same way again. And I knew Eli was to blame.

~NATE FINLAY~

THERE. SHE KNEW. I couldn't keep it in any longer. Knowing she had fought and won against cancer since we'd last seen one another made me feel like an even bigger bastard for pretending not to remember her. She remained quiet about it. Not reminding me. Not trying to get me to remember her. Most girls would've been upset and dramatic, needing to draw attention.

Not Bliss. She said nothing at all. Did her job and smiled when I made her. The joy that had originally drawn me to her was still there as if it never left. Even after all she'd been through. I was the world's biggest jackass. I intended to rectify that. If it was humanly possible I would.

"Who told you?" Finally, she spoke the words. She'd been staring at me for a while, as if she wasn't sure what to say, or if she'd heard me correctly. There was sadness. She didn't want me to know. But why? Perhaps I didn't deserve to.

"Does that matter?"

She nodded. "Yes. It does."

"Bliss, let's go, we're going to be late," Eli called out to her. She didn't look at him or speak. There was a flash of anger in her eyes and I realized she was mad at Eli.

"He didn't tell me," I replied, although I don't know why. I kind of liked the idea of her being angry with him over something like that. He fit so perfectly into her life. Eli was able to be with her through every moment of the day if he chose to. I wasn't. I hadn't been given a Bliss. I'd chosen, instead, an Octavia.

"Then who?" she asked again, this time with obvious anger in her voice. It was sexy, she was never angry, or hell, never even ornery. She made "pissed off" look good.

"My grandfather. He thought I knew and mentioned it, while

we were eating at his place."

Her anger quickly faded. The sadness was back in an instant. She stood there for a moment bewildered. "Okay," she whispered, turning to leave, but I couldn't let her go. "Wait," I called after Bliss. She knew the truth that I'd been a lying asshole and she hadn't even mentioned it. I needed more. A slap in the face? She could yell at me if she chose to.

She paused and with an obvious sigh turned back to me to speak.

"I'm sorry," was all I could say. I was, more so than I'd ever been for anything I'd ever done.

"For what?"

Did she actually have to ask me that? I would've thought the reason was obvious. I had a mountain of shit to be sorry for. "For letting you believe I didn't remember you. I thought it was for the best. But it was wrong. A cruel thing to do."

"Oh. I just thought I was forgettable." She shrugged her shoulders and tilted her head. "That was a million years ago. We've both lived another life since then."

She'd survived through a hell that changed her. Robbing Bliss of experiences she should have had, yet she didn't complain in the least. "I'd like to know the woman you've become. We were friends once, before I kissed you. We could be friends again."

As I said the words I realized I didn't have that many real friends. The relationship she had with Eli was unique. That, I had with no one. Lila Kate and I could've had that. If our mothers hadn't intended us to marry. We'd never gotten too close. Our mothers' hopes would rise if we did.

Octavia wasn't my friend. We didn't talk about much. She talked about her store, parties to attend and the wedding, stuff like that. The way Bliss and I talked yesterday at my grandpops was a thing I wanted more of. That could be asking for trouble.

A fucking load of trouble, but I wanted it.

"I don't think that's possible Nate." Her voice was soft as she said it and it waivered as if she didn't want to say or believe her own words. Then she left me standing there. Watching her go.

Eli was waiting at his truck. The look on his face said it all. She may see him as a friend, but he saw her as more than that. I believed he always had. There was a possessiveness in his stance. The way he held her door and watched me. Waiting to see if I spoke.

I met his gaze and the warning was clear. He was staking his claim silently. Just for me. I understood it. That made more sense than what Bliss believed they were. A girl like that didn't have a guy as "just a friend" not when you looked like Bliss. Any fucking man would want more from her. She was the perfect package of beauty and innocence, nothing ugly about her; inside or out, and you could see it.

Other than Bliss I'd never seen that combination in a woman and trust me, I've looked. A lot. More than I should have. After my summer with her I measured every female by her standards. Until I convinced myself that what I was remembering was an illusion, because we're all imperfect. I let it go and the line of beauties that followed had little more than unbelievable bodies. That was their selling point.

Octavia was a drama free selection. Easy, unchallenging and simple. She had been a relief. What I thought I was looking for. Until I came back here. Until I saw Bliss again. Then I remembered what perfect actually was. What I wouldn't have. What I had once had.

Eli opened the door for her and I watched as she climbed inside. He spoke to Bliss, she only nodded, Eli quickly closing the door. Again, he looked at me. If Bliss were anyone else I'd take that as a challenge. I'd win. I always did. But this wasn't a game

I would play.

She was what I knew I couldn't touch. My world wasn't for her. She was Sea Breeze and her world was here. Mine was out there waiting. Getting the hell out of one coastal town and settling in another wasn't change. It was another fucking coastal town.

What I wanted was Bliss's friendship. Being friends with her would be the hardest damn thing I ever did but I could do it. Eli was what Bliss needed. I was made for the Octavia's of the world. No matter what my mom believed. She had other ideas concerning me. I didn't have the heart to tell her how off she was about her son.

I was my father's son. But there wouldn't be a Blaire to save me. I wasn't open to that. Bliss wasn't going to change me. Just for this summer I'd like for her to be exactly as she was back then. To feel truly happy, full of hope, and alive as I'd once remembered. Life became dark at times. Bliss knew that better than anyone. Yet, she lived with a smile, maintained that hope in her eyes. For three months I could enjoy it.

Getting past Eli was the problem. He didn't trust me. Didn't even like me. I thought about how much he'd hated me seven years ago. Bliss had been naïve, hadn't seen it. I did and hadn't cared.

Chapter Eight

♥ BLISS YORK ♥

"**I**S HE EVER going to realize she doesn't like him?" Crimson disgustedly asked as she came to stand beside me. I searched for Cruz knowing it was him we were discussing without any explanation. He was, as always, talking to Hadley. Poor boy was fixated on her.

Hadley had flown in on her father's private jet with her parents and sister for this party. In the morning they'd return to their home in Beverly Hills. In June, they'd come back, to yet another house, the one here they occupied for the summer. She lived a life so distant from any of ours that none of us was close to her.

"He has to try," I replied. The real issue here was that Crimson had, as of late, become interested in Cruz . . . again. It wasn't the first time. When they were little they were inseparable. Much like Eli and me. But Crimson had always had stars in her eyes whenever she was around him. Time had changed them both, but the stars were still there for Crimson. Cruz led the terrible six. It took a lot to keep them constantly in trouble. Crimson was too smart for that. Or I thought she was.

"He's the son of my father. Or so my momma says. So be

careful Crimson. He's not the settling down type. I love him, don't get me wrong, but he's in it for women period. All women. Every single one."

Crimson sighed and growled frustratingly. "Yeah, that's what my mom says, but your dad settled down for your mother. It is possible. Anything is."

"You're nineteen. Don't even think about settling down yet."

She shrugged. "I don't think it sounds so bad."

Crimson believed the fantasy. The one her parents had as did mine. I wanted that but I wondered if it was possible anymore. Did people still love like they did? Had that become a thing of the past?

"I want a fairytale," she said softly.

I replied "Crimson, we all do" and put my arm around her shoulder. "But Cruz isn't the one. Keep looking."

She nodded. "Yeah, I know."

"What are y'all whispering about?" Saffron asked as she sauntered up to us. Her skirt was so short if she bent over her bottom would show.

"How long everyone is going to pretend that Larissa and Micah aren't dating. My guess is by Christmas we will all admit to knowing their secret. Unless Preston figures it out. Then their cover is blown." I said that to conceal Crimson's issue from Saffron who couldn't keep her mouth closed. If she got wind of Crimson liking Cruz then it would be her mission to have him. Although she'd already been there and done that.

"I thought they were awfully close," Saffron whispered as her eyes got big. Micah and Larissa would kill me if this got back to them. I'd made that up to get Saffron off the scent of a challenge, any obstacle, because she liked to take guys from other girls. Then she would throw them away.

The constant chatter of my "family" that surrounded me helped distract me from the conversation I'd had with Nate.

Tonight as I lay in bed I would have time to go over it. He wanted to be friends. Friends? My chest hurt every time that word rang in my ears. Of course that was all he could want. He was engaged. And SHE was my boss.

How was I supposed to be friends with him? I needed to date again. That was my problem. My hurdle. Nate held a special place in my heart because he was my best relationship. The best I had experienced. After him no one had met my expectations. But I'd only been fifteen. We were kids being dreamy and irrational.

I had to try some more. The few dates I'd been on hadn't been that great but that didn't mean they were bad. I needed to test the waters. Take chances with different personalities; anything to wash Nate's memory from my dreams, both day and night, because our time together plagued me.

"I've got to go in the back and get Cleo off the phone. Quickly, before my dad sees." Crimson then excused herself to find her sister.

Saffron saw Holland talking to James Stone and hurried over there to draw attention, knowing she didn't like James. She just wanted his eyes on her.

"What's going on in that head of yours?" my mother asked as she walked over to me, holding out a cup of punch. "I've watched you all evening. You're upset about something. That frown line gives you away."

I took the punch from her. I could lie but she would know. Momma knew everything. So, I was honest. "Nate Finlay is engaged to my boss."

Mom's eyes went wide. "The boy from that summer?"

I nodded. "Yep, the same."

"Oh my," she whispered and her frown matched mine. After all I had inherited it from her.

"Yeah, 'oh my' is right."

"How long have you known?" she asked.

"Since the very first day at work. I didn't think he remembered me. He pretended not to until this afternoon . . ."

Mom looked mad and interrupted. "Jerk. Goodness. That's rude."

I had to laugh. Momma was like talking to a friend. She listened and didn't try to sugar coat it. We'd faced my cancer together. That made your bond stronger and I thought we were closer, as near to one another as could be.

"He wants to be friends," I said.

She released a short laugh, as if that were ridiculous and I had to agree with her. At least she wasn't telling me to give it a try, because my mom was honest and realistic. I loved that about her.

"He's engaged. You can't be friends. That's impossible."

I nodded.

"Does Eli know?"

I wasn't sure why she asked that. There was no reason for Eli to know. He would just get overprotective and I wasn't in the mood for that.

"No. He'll worry."

"He loves you."

"I love him."

Momma gave a sad smile. "I know." I could tell by the look on her face she wanted to say more but she didn't. Instead she took my hand and squeezed it. "One day you'll know more."

That didn't make sense to me. Momma often said things that didn't. Like she wanted me to figure life out on my own. I didn't push for an explanation. Sometimes I did, but this time I didn't, my gut telling me "you don't want to know." Right now I had enough to deal with. Like the fact that I knew being Nate Finlay's friend was a terrible idea from the start. Yet, I was going to do it. Because if I didn't, I would always wonder "what if it had just been a friendship? It could've been one like Eli's." I knew I was lying to myself. But cancer had taught me a lot. And the "what if's" of this world were something I decided I never wanted to have. I wasn't about to begin with Nate.

~NATE FINLAY~

I WAS LATE coming into work because it had taken me three cups of coffee and about ten pep talks to get me out the damn door. Facing Bliss today wasn't going to be easy. She hadn't left me yesterday on a good note. She'd been hurt and angry.

When I opened the back door and heard the familiar voice of my youngest sister talking I froze. What the hell was Phoenix doing here? She was supposed to be in school. Last time I checked she was still a senior. Graduation wasn't for two more weeks. Bliss laughed and I stalked toward their voices. I didn't trust Phoenix not to say a bunch of shit she shouldn't. The girl was an annoying loud mouth.

"... and then we had to tell dad. Ophelia didn't have enough money for bail ..." Phoenix finished with her cup of coffee in hand as she gestured theatrically with her other. Both females began to laugh.

I'd never seen my sisters laugh with Octavia. She wasn't much of a laugher herself. She thought my sisters were silly. I had to agree with her. However, seeing Phoenix so at ease with Bliss was nice. Too damn nice to be comfortable.

"Hate to break up the party but what the hell are you doing here? Why aren't you in school?"

Phoenix didn't even jump at the sound of my voice. "Good to see you to big brother. Hope you're doing well. Yes, I am wonderful. Ready for finals and oh, of course, I'm registered at Washington State."

I rolled my eyes. This was how Phoenix got the subject off her and made you feel guilty in the process. It worked with most of my family. Not me. Never had.

"I didn't ask about any of that shit. Why aren't you in school? Why are you here?"

She turned her attention back to Bliss. "He's rude. Always has been."

Bliss softly giggled. This morning I arrived ready to convince her to be a friend to me. Why, I wasn't sure, because it was probably a stupid idea. But I wanted it nonetheless, like asking to be punched again. And after hours of talking myself into acting, I arrive to find my freaking sister here. Screwing it up for me.

"I need to get back to the window display. I'll leave you two to visit." Bliss spoke, then stood, walking away and though I shouldn't watch her walk, I did because I was a man.

"Well, I'll be damned," Phoenix said, snapping my attention back to her.

"What?"

She smirked and looked at Bliss's back then cut her eyes at me. "Please tell me that she," Phoenix threw her chin at Bliss "has the ability to end this ridiculous relationship you have with Octavia."

It wasn't just my mom who didn't care for Octavia. It was all the women in my life.

"Octavia's been nothing but nice to you," I reminded her. She had been nice to all of them.

"Nice, but uppity," she replied. "There's always a snarl beneath it."

We lived in a world of uppity with snarls. I didn't point that out. I decided to let it go.

"Why are you here?" I asked more firmly this time. I was close to calling dad. Phoenix didn't want that.

"Because," she said with a sigh "a few of the graduating class hung our underwear on the flagpole. That was the night before last. Alcohol may have been involved. It seemed hilarious at the time. Even the next morning at school. Until we found out there were security cameras. We should've known that beforehand. Anyway, today they'll be calling our parents. So I'm hiding. What are you up to?" She ended it so casually.

The flagpole thing was stupid, not criminal. Hell, I'd done a lot worse when I was a student there. "Go home and face it Phoenix. Mom will remind him that he's getting paid back for the sins of his younger years. You're the baby. He'll calm down. They always let you get away with shit."

Phoenix frowned. "I was drunk in the security footage. That's why they'll go bananas."

Agreed. They'd be furious. But she wasn't hiding here forever. I had my own shit to deal with. Octavia would be back soon. I had to get my head on straight before she walked in the door.

"Stop drinking. It leads to stupid shit. Wait until you're legal then make your mistakes. Now go home and get it over with."

She pouted. "Please go with me."

I glanced over at Bliss working in the window. Normally when Phoenix needed me I was there without delay. She was, after all, the baby. And we babied the shit out of her. That was the reason she was wild as a buck. Even Ophelia bailed her out of trouble. Took the blame for things she shouldn't.

"I can't."

Phoenix released a defeated sigh. "Normally, now, I'd commence the waterworks and cry until you caved. But I love you and will refrain. And if that girl Bliss can remove your head from Octavia's uptown ass, where it seems to have been lodged for months, then good, that's what I want. Even more than our parents assaulting me and burying my body in the sand."

I rolled my eyes. How fucking dramatic. "For starters, my head is free of all asses and has never been in Octavia's. Secondly, our folks aren't exactly the toughest parents in Rosemary."

She shrugged and stood without worry.

"I'm going to enjoy the day here. Walk on the beach where people don't know me and eat some lunch like a stranger. Then, after they've worried, I'll call and head home in shambles. Maybe their relief that I haven't washed up on the beach or been drawn into a sex racket, will make them forget about the punishment."

I doubted it and figured it would only make it worse but I wanted her to leave so I nodded. Truth was if they called me frantic I was telling them where she was. I didn't want my momma to worry. Dad would worry, but he'd be pissed, and wouldn't care about her emotional wellbeing.

"See you in a week Phoenix. I'll be home for graduation."

She kissed my cheek then headed for the door. "Bye Bliss! Lovely meeting you! Would be even lovelier if you . . ."

"Phoenix!" I stopped the comment.

She threw her head back and laughed, then sashayed out the door.

Life with two younger sisters had never been easy. Dad said it was why I was patient, with women and animals and old people. He had raised my Aunt Nan, said it taught him a lot, Phoenix often compared to her in looks and personality. She wasn't as mean as they say Nan was, but then she had a stable life growing up. Aunt Nan hadn't had that. Until Uncle Cope came along she was a destructive and angry hot mess. Or at least that's the story I've heard.

I turned my attention back to Bliss and the way she was studying the window. Her intensity reminded me of a moment seven years ago. It was then that I realized she was special and I wouldn't be able to forget her.

She must have felt my gaze. Bliss paused and looked directly at me. Her eyes met mine and she smiled. As if she knew what I was thinking and she remembered it too and while remembering turned to me.

SEVEN YEARS AGO . . .

She was worried about her friend. He was home from basketball camp. She'd convinced her parents to let her stay another week at the beach with Larissa, who had helped with that, because her parents were constantly fretting. Eli, however, wasn't real happy about her being with me all the time.

I woke up and headed for our spot on the beach every morning around the same time. Quite often she was there first. Others days I beat her there. At night we texted on the phone until she stopped which meant she'd fallen asleep.

This summer was a hell of a lot better than I ever imagined it being. I wasn't sure I wanted to go back to Rosemary Beach next month. I liked my grandpop's condo and the food at his bar, the way this beach was touristy, but not so exclusive and elitist like it was at home. And well, if I was being absolutely fucking honest, I liked Bliss York and was pretty sure I was in love. She ruled my thoughts.

I watched her as she watched Eli walk away. We'd been standing in line at the ice cream stand when he came up to her to talk. Asked if she wanted to go surfing with him and someone I didn't know named Micah. She had declined and he'd glared at me, before walking away with his shoulders drooping, doing that defeated thing.

"Maybe I should have gone. We both could have gone." Her frown was so damn sweet it hurt. Of course I had to add stark reality.

"I wasn't invited Bliss."

She inhaled and exhaled deeply then turned back to me. *"That's because he doesn't know you Nate. He has to warm up to you."*

No, that wasn't correct. It was because her friend was jealous. I saw it, understood it, but I wasn't about to let her leave me for him. If she really wanted I'd let her go, but not because that pussy pouted and retreated like a ten-year old child.

"I could go do something else. Catch up with you later," I replied. I tried to sound cool, like I was fine with that, but I knew this was a gamble. She could easily agree and walk off. But the way I scanned the area, as if searching for someone to hang with, was the card I was playing at that moment.

"No," she said quickly. *"I want to stay with you."*

I turned back to her and smiled. She felt it to. I knew it. I wasn't alone in this. The girl who had gotten under my skin was feeling it just like me. Why she liked me when a girl like her fit best with an Eli was beyond me. I wasn't sure, but damn I was lucky.

"Good," I replied. *"You make being here worth it."*

The smile that lit her face made me want to say all kinds of mushy shit. Just to see that smile again, and again and again and again . . .

Chapter Nine

♥ BLISS YORK ♥

"HAVE YOU FORGIVEN me for lying?" was the first thing he said when his sister left. I was relieved Phoenix had been here. It kept us from having this conversation long enough to get my head together.

"Yes," I replied, because I had. I understood why he did it. It didn't feel good but I got it.

"And have you thought about us being friends?"

He wasn't wasting time getting to the point. But then Nate Finlay never had. The truth was there waiting and he dealt with it. It was best this got done before Octavia returned. That was probably what he was thinking at the moment.

"We have to work together. I mean you'll be here helping Octavia. I don't see why we shouldn't be friends. It would make things run a little easier."

He frowned. That hadn't been the answer he was looking for. Well, what was? What did he want me to say? Yes! Let's go get ice cream then kiss under the bridge like we used to? That memory stung deep. I shoved it down. Way down. Those memories weren't available anymore. They couldn't be unpacked and toyed with.

Not if I was going to get over him.

"Octavia will be here in the next few days . . . and . . . I have questions about the past and you . . . your illness . . . how you overcame it."

Well boo-hoo. I bet he did. That didn't mean I was going to open up and share with him. I didn't want him to know. In my head, I wanted us to remain the way we were, which was stupid, because I had no future with Nate. I suppose, I had no real reason not to tell him, except I didn't want to, didn't have to, and would do whatever I chose. Not be pressed into telling because he carried some guilt and needed that burden lifted.

"I don't talk about it," I replied and continued working on the window. I had to find a way to make the scarves fit with the summer display I'd arranged. This was south Alabama. It was scorching hot in the summer. Octavia needed to remember that when she went buying stuff to sell. We both had a lot to learn and I appreciated her hiring me.

"Why?" he asked. "Why not get it off your chest?"

I rolled my eyes. Yes, I was acting like a teenager. He wanted to know something I didn't want to talk to him about so he was going to ask me why. Did he think he'd get me to open up? Talk about it? Because he was being nosey? I'd been there and done that with plenty of people and wasn't doing that with him.

"Because Nate. Simply BECAUSE."

He became silent. Good. He needed to get on with his work for the day and I needed to do the same.

"You didn't answer my texts or calls. I tried. Made the effort. It wasn't me who turned you away."

I closed my eyes tightly and sighed. He wasn't letting this go. We were going to have to discuss it. Get it out in the open and deal. Which was ridiculous. We'd been kids. I had handled it the way a teenage girl knew to handle things.

"I was facing the scariest thing imaginable. What else do you need to know? I wasn't in the frame of mind to keep up with a childhood crush." That was a little harsh, but it was the truth and the truth can sting.

"But I thought we were more than that?"

Maybe we had been. Maybe it was my fault. I'd been confronted with something that changed me. And when I was ready to tell him it had been too late. Too much time had passed and I was different, so very different. My fairytale life had ended. The real world had slapped me in the face. A loving family and a stable home with all the support on earth, can't save you from something like cancer. It only deals in darkness and pain. You defeat it or it defeats you. Until you experience it you don't understand the depth of it

I folded the scarf and looked to him. "I was too scared to think about boys. About friendships or the drama of people. Because I wasn't sure I had a future beyond my next doctor's visit. I woke up one day with my life all planned to look a certain way. It had been so exciting, so full of dreams, but then in one doctor's consult I was told that I had cancer. That my life wasn't guaranteed. Nothing was ever the same and it won't ever be."

Nate kept his gaze on me. There wasn't pity or fear that it could happen to him, beneath the silver pools of his eyes. I saw those two things a lot, pity and fear in people. Not seeing them in his eyes was a relief. It would have hurt. Let me down. But like I'd always known Nate was different. He wasn't like the other boys.

He still saw me. Most people didn't. They just saw the disease inside me. The one I had beaten, yet that seemed to remain in their minds after it was gone. I wanted to hug him for that. Thank him and rely on his judgment for that not to be weird and out of place. But he wouldn't understand. He hadn't lived what I had been through.

"I would've come back here. I'd have probably moved in with my grandpop to be close to you if I'd known."

It hadn't been meant to be that way. He loved his parents and sisters, his life in Rosemary Beach and it was there that he needed to stay. He belonged with them and not me. Him coming here wouldn't have been good for Nate or his family. My guilt, over that, wouldn't have helped my fight, and back then I fought every minute.

"We were kids. Things happen. We become different people. It's the past now, let's just leave it."

Nate studied me intensely without looking away or trying to argue some point. I could see his mind working right there in the steadiness of his gaze and stance. When he finally released a sigh he nodded and said "okay." That was all he said.

I didn't want him to see the disappointment in my eyes so I turned back to the window. My mind was no longer focused on my work. He had agreed. He hadn't argued. I should be relieved. The fact I wanted him to argue was silly. Childish and I wasn't childish, not anymore I wasn't.

I listened as he walked away. I heard the back door open and close. I squeezed my eyes tightly together wishing the ache in my chest would vanish. Leave me be for a while. Give me some peace and tranquility.

I was finally free, living on my own and had a grown-up life. Being sad was pointless now. I had so much to be happy about. I wanted that happiness I saw on other faces and wishing for something far from my reach was wasting time and effort. I knew how fleeting time could be, because I'd almost run completely out.

Once I thought that the scripture in the Bible about not being promised tomorrow was depressing and lacked any joy. Now I knew it was real. Something we all needed to accept. I did, so why was I wasting it on wishing Nate Finlay was tomorrow, the tomorrow I would claim as my future? Instead of just being my past?

~NATE FINLAY~

I DIDN'T INTEND to stay in the back all morning. But I had. I wanted to think about what she'd said and figure out how to deal with her. I should agree and accept her suggestion. If I had more time to think about it, I knew I would have changed my mind.

But I didn't.

Ten minutes before I was going to get Bliss and take her to lunch again Octavia came barreling in the back door with her arms full of shopping bags and a huge smile on her face.

Shit. This was too soon. I wasn't ready for her yet. Which should've been a sign I acknowledged. Wanting her to stay away.

"The window looks amazing. She's brilliant. Didn't I tell you I'd found a perfect match for the store, a girl that knew what she was doing? She's also easy to train. Not old and snooty. She does what I say and doesn't question me. I like her." Those were the first words out of her mouth after not seeing me for almost a month.

Until I returned to Sea Breeze and saw Bliss this was normal. Exactly what I wanted. It was easy, without drama, and there was no real attachment. Fuck this place and my stupid memories. What I had was perfect.

"Haven't seen her window display yet. I've been back here installing the shelves you ordered."

She frowned as she looked at the shelves. "Not as big as I had imagined."

Octavia needed a handy man or had to make it easier for me. All she had to do was measure correctly and she would always have the proper size. I could tell her that but then she'd get pissy and have me pack it back up.

"I'll just order a few more sets I suppose," she said with a wave of her hand, as if this were an easy fix and she had no time to stress over it. I wondered how long this was going to entertain her? When it would become boring and she would walk away and want something else to sustain her, another fucking whim she'd abandon? Her father always granted her wishes. This was just another expedition, Octavia would eventually ignore.

The name of the store should be Whimsy's or Whimsical or Octavia's . . . I Don't Really Care. That was all this was. She'd never admit that was true. When you're enabled and rescued time and again you don't have to look at yourself. It's like a mirror without any glass. All you see is your next big screw up.

"I'm starving. Have you found anywhere good to eat?"

"My grandpops," was my response. She knew it would be. Just like I knew she would scrunch her nose in distaste.

"No thanks. I'll Google it. Go wash up and let's take Bliss to have a decent lunch. I need to keep her around."

"Bliss likes grandpops," I shot back. That was asking for trouble. But damn if Octavia didn't suddenly annoy me and it only took twenty fucking minutes.

She didn't even turn back. "Of course she does. She's simple."

Then she walked through the door to the front of the store, her high and mighty completely intact.

Bliss wasn't simple. Not by a long shot.

I went to the restroom, washed my hands then stared at myself in the mirror. I needed mental preparation for this. To remind myself why I chose Octavia and why Bliss wasn't a fit. I had no place in my heart or future for all that Bliss would require. And if I admitted that . . . the idea that I could let myself love her and then have her cancer come back, scared the shit out of me.

That would break me into pieces. I wasn't willing to be broken or made that vulnerable, which was selfish and all about my safety, the most fucking selfish thought I'd ever had and I was pretty damn sure I'd had plenty. But it was true and I accepted my truths. I didn't pretend to be noble. At least not anymore . . .

SEVEN YEARS AGO . . .

I was early. Bliss told me to meet her at our spot on the beach around ten this morning. It was nine thirty. I didn't want her to get here before me. Not after yesterday. She'd let me kiss her and it was hands down the best kiss I'd ever had. Not that I'd had that many. And I wasn't counting Lila Kate. Neither one of us had kissed anyone before three years ago when we decided to practice on one other. It grossed us both out. Like kissing a sibling. Didn't happen again.

Kissing Bliss had been amazing. She smelled like the coconut in her tanning oil along with something else. It was unique to her and I couldn't get enough of it. When I leaned in to kiss her last night I was afraid she'd push me away. She hadn't. She'd slipped her hands up my arms and linked her fingers behind my neck. It'd been hard to let go after that.

So this morning I'm waiting on her. Making sure she knew that the kiss meant a lot, that she was special and that I loved her. I hadn't really thought love was possible until you were older and experienced. I realized I was wrong. My heart was so damn tight when I looked at her that it ached when she walked away. I wasn't sure there was any definitive thing that could explain what love was. To me this was my definition.

"You're Nate Finlay aren't you?" I turned to see a girl whose body advertised that she was at least eighteen. Her boobs were about to spill from her bikini. They were the biggest I'd seen close up. Her long blonde hair was thrown over her shoulder and the tanned skin she so generously exposed was shiny with oil and early sweat. If I hadn't grown up on a beach then this might be exciting. But I was a Finlay and in my world I had this in my face quite often, especially at the country club.

I wasn't sure how the girl knew my name. I shrugged my shoulders and glanced back down the beach looking for Bliss with urgency. "Yeah, but I don't know you."

She giggled and I cringed. I didn't like the gigglers. They annoyed the shit out of me. Bliss didn't do the flirty giggle thing. Two years back that was the primary reason Bliss became attractive to me. Of course, after raw beauty.

"My grandparents are members of The Kerrington Club. I normally spend a month each summer in Rosemary Beach with them. I've seen you there."

The two beaches were only two and a half hours apart. But seriously, the place had to follow me here? Jesus.

"Well now," *I replied.* "Now you see me here." *I tried my hardest to sound like an asshole so she'd leave before Bliss got here. I didn't need her walking up to me while talking to Miss Big Tits, especially after last night's kiss.*

She did the giggle again. "Yes, I do. Want to sit with my friends and I? I saw you yesterday with the young girl and pointed you out to them. They're fascinated that your grandfather is Dean Finlay."

My dad's dad is the famous drummer for Slacker Demon. They're the iconic rock band that was now retired for the most part. They'd become grandfathers and the new generation wasn't to their liking. When asked they came together for fundraisers, but that was the extent of their performances. Still though, there were the worshippers. They had a lifetime of fame that spanned three generations of fans that would never forget them.

"Most people are," *I replied. And just as I said those words Bliss's dark hair came into view. She was walking this way somewhat casually. The simple white lace cover-up she wore over her hot pink bikini didn't show nearly as much body, compared to this other girl. Bliss looked classy and sure of herself. She had the brain to go with everything else.* "Excuse me, my girl is here," *I said without looking back. I then headed to meet Bliss in my eagerness. Had I been another guy, one who wasn't in love with Bliss York then I'd gone the other route. She would've been my first and I would've enjoyed every moment of losing my virginity. I knew that, but no, not now, she wasn't what I was looking for.*

Chapter Ten

♥ BLISS YORK ♥

LUNCH WITH NATE and Octavia. Great. Just what I
wanted to do. Never.

Sitting across from them at some fancy lunch place that
I didn't even know was in Sea Breeze I tried to keep a polite smile
and I didn't make eye contact with Nate. Which was difficult when
I could feel his steady gaze on me. Watching me. Trying to read
something into my expressions. I was easy to read. I hated that.
Knowing he could see how uncomfortable I was.

"I like the way you incorporated the scarf into the summer
pieces I've chosen. It works and it's exactly what I had in mind.
You have an eye for this thing. We just need to get you into the
clothing. Your wardrobe doesn't fit with the look of the place. But
with your body advertising the inventory then we will sell more."

In other words, my clothes were too cheap. My momma had
always bought me designer clothing. I had never been accused of
not being stylish. However, compared to Octavia I might as well
be wearing clothes from a thrift store. She had another level of
acceptable. I had seen the price tags on the items she bought for

the store. I imagined her closet was full of similar items.

"I'm open to whatever you need me to do," I assured her. I was thankful I had this job. It gave me my independence and I was finally able to live like an adult. Not a kid.

She flashed a very white glamorous smile my way and I wondered how much that smile had cost. There was no way those teeth were real. They were too white, too straight, too perfect. My braces hadn't even given me those straight lines.

"Now that the summer line is in and I've chosen everything, I'll give it a couple weeks then begin buying for the fall. It's still warm here then so I'll keep that in mind." I wasn't sure who she was talking to, me, Nate or herself. But she continued to rattle on about profit and design and expanding. She hadn't even been officially open yet and she was talking about opening five other stores within the US. I wouldn't be surprised if she started planning her stores in other countries before the salads got to the table.

"The tourist arrive here the first week in June?" Octavia asked as she looked at me.

"Yes sometimes sooner. We start to see more traffic the last week in May. Depends on when schools let out in the surrounding states."

She nodded and the waiter arrived with our salads. I took a peek at Nate and he was frowning at his salad in disgust. I assumed he was used to places like this. I knew his lifestyle outside of Sea Breeze was very different.

"A shrimp poboy would have been a helluva lot better than this," he grumbled.

Octavia rolled her eyes with an amused smile. "You'd have those shrimp poboys at or wedding reception if I let you. What is a poboy anyway? Why call them that? It's so degrading. Why not just call them a hoagie. It's what they are."

A hoagie? What was a hoagie?

"Jesus," he muttered but that was the only response he was giving her.

"I see you two have worked well together," Octavia said as she went to take a bite of her salad.

I froze. What did she mean? I hadn't been looking at Nate or even saying anything about him. I'd been very careful. Had his staring at me gave it away? Dangit Nate! I needed this job.

"She's a hard worker. You hired well," Nate said then took one of the long toasted pieces of bread that came with our salads and shoved it in his mouth.

Octavia cocked an eyebrow at him as if she wasn't thrilled with the way he was eating then turned to me. "Agreed. I can tell you're going to be easy to work with. I like you and I don't like people easily. You've got that something about you that people are drawn to and that will only help the store. I need the store to flourish so daddy will let me continue with more Octavia's."

A part of me felt admiration for her. A very, very small part. She wanted to do something with her life. Make a mark. Be more than a socialite and I admired that. You had to. I saw so many like her on the news and media that were just living off their parents wealth. Sure, Octavia was also living off her father's fortune but she was trying to make a fortune herself. He was just her stepping stool. . . . Or her very high ladder. Or her private jet. It wouldn't be too hard to make a success with the money she had to play with. But still. She was trying. That counted for something.

I wasn't much better. I'd lived with my parents well past the age I should have. I had let them feed me and put a roof over my head. And buy me a car, and buy my clothing . . . it was all on a much smaller scale but in comparison it was the same.

"Nate won't be here much and I will need to travel once we

get things going. So, it will be on you to handle everything soon. I believe you can do that. We will look into hiring two other employees to work under you before I leave for Spain at the end of the month. Nate will more than likely be back in Rosemary Beach or in Beverly Hills by then. But I feel confident I can trust you."

Why would Nate be in Beverly Hills? He hated it there. Other than visiting his other grandfather he tried to go there as little as possible. I glanced at him and he was watching me again. I only met his eyes briefly before dropping them back to my salad.

"Thank you," I told Octavia. "I'll do my best."

"Great."

After we returned to the store I made myself busy in the front. Although my thoughts stayed on how odd Octavia and Nate were with each other. There was no connection of any kind. They seemed annoyed by the other. Did he realize that?

Just as I began to wonder if I should say something to him before he made a mistake and married her I heard laughter. I paused and listened. It was both of them. Their voices mingled as they laughed. Setting down the dress in my hand I walked quietly over to the door. It was wrong to eavesdrop but I did it anyway. They were laughing and that seemed so out of place after watching them together.

"I love your stories," Octavia said with a hint of amusement still in her voice.

"It's a gift," he replied.

"Hmmm, one of the many reasons I love you," was her response then the distinct sound of kissing followed. It wasn't loud. It was just the sound of bodies pressed close. Breathing erratic and choppy, and silence when there had been talking.

I stepped back. Eavesdropping was never a good thing and those who did it deserved to be punished. This was my punishment.

~NATE FINLAY~

I MADE EXCUSES to stay away from Octavia's for three days. The more distance I could put between Bliss and I the better things would be for all three of us. Octavia was back and that was enough to remind me what I needed in a life. What fit me and was safe, because being near Bliss was not safe. Just being in a room with Bliss wasn't safe. She tempted me with a life I didn't want.

Each evening I listened to Octavia talk about Bliss's ideas for the store. I took her out to dinner to the places she chose and was supportive without intervening. I did the things I normally did. However, when she asked to go listen to a band on Friday night at Live Bay I paused. That was a bad idea. More than likely Bliss would be there. Dating Octavia with Bliss watching wasn't okay with me. If the situation were reversed it wouldn't be easy for me to watch her with another guy. I didn't think it was fair to Bliss. Even if she'd moved on and was over what we had or what we thought we had in the past, rubbing the other's face in that history seemed cruel.

I tried talking Octavia into going somewhere else. She was dead set on Live Bay and checking out the local scene. Octavia said she needed some "down time," like there was any real stress heaped upon her. Mixing with the "regular people" here would help her "release the tension that comes with being a success."

There was a chance Bliss had other plans. That's what I held onto until Octavia shot that to hell. We were entering Live Bay when Octavia stopped. She scanned the crowd like a Secret Service agent: "Bliss said her table was to the left near the bar and that she's saving us a spot."

This was one small piece of information that Octavia failed to mention. She must have not considered it important. I gazed at

Bliss's table and there she was, sitting in some guy's lap, laughing with a drink in her hand. That was nothing like Bliss and he was older than me. What the fuck? Why was I here?

"There she is," Octavia announced. She then slipped her arm through mine. Drug me towards the pair like a child.

I then tried to think of a logical excuse to get me the hell out of there. Trusting myself not to do something stupid wasn't easy with Bliss flirtingly drunk and lap wiggling on older guys. Where was fucking Eli? Jesus!

"Y'all came!" Bliss beamed and jumped up. "I hoped you would but I wasn't positive. Here, take those seats."

She didn't sound drunk, but was too damn happy about this unfolding before her. "Everyone, this is my boss Octavia and her fiancé Nate Finlay!" She then looked back at us. "That's Jimmy," she pointed to the guy whose lap she'd been perched on wiggling and laughing. I glared at Jimmy who returned a smug smile then drank from his whiskey glass. "That's Micah, Daisy May, James and Crimson" Bliss said, going in a circle, like we were at a book study group. Oddly, none of them appeared to be couples, which was weird and wasn't lost on me.

"I'm just here to take care of Saffron whenever she appears," said the girl Crimson, with an annoyed look and a huff.

Bliss added "Saffron is a bit of a handful. What do y'all want to drink?"

"Grey Goose martini," Octavia replied.

"Maker's Mark is fine," I told her.

She waved her hand towards the bartender. "Larissa, we need a Grey Goose martini and a Maker's Mark, please."

The red head shot her thumbs up and went to work. I knew she looked familiar the last time I was in here. Hearing Bliss say her name I remembered why that was. Larissa was the girl who brought Bliss to the beach that summer long ago. Glancing around at the others, I wondered if I'd met them before.

As if he could read my mind Micah pointed his beer at me: "Nate Finlay? Damn, you look familiar!"

We'd met once, I remembered his face as well, but he didn't need to figure that out right here in front of Octavia. We'd have a shit ton of explaining to do. Octavia knew nothing at all. The less she knew the better, as far as I was concerned.

"His grandfather is famous," Octavia replied. "When he was younger Nate's father was in the media a lot. They look like twins I swear. It's freaky to see them together."

Micah started to shake his head no. Bliss walked over, grabbed his hand, and blurted out "Micah, you promised me a dance. Let's dance now . . . right now."

Micah looked confused, but he didn't turn her down. I doubt any man would. He stood and stretched like he'd be jumping hurdles: "I like it when you're bossy and shit. Do it more. Make me mind."

He was grinning like it was a joke. It really pissed me off. Bliss, however, laughed and tugged his arm, so he followed her willingly to the dance floor.

"Drinks are ready," Jimmy said, nodding his head toward the bar. I needed an escape so I took it. "I'll get them," I replied, before bolting the scene, getting away from the pack and keeping my eyes off Bliss, especially while she danced. That seemed an important task. Not to watch her body move.

When I got to the bar the gorgeous red head stopped mixing and looked directly at my face. "They don't remember Nate, but I do."

Shit. What do I say to that? She sat down her shaker, walked over to me, until she was as close as she could get. Still, she leaned aggressively forward, only the bar separating us. "She's been through a hell we can't imagine. You hurt her and those guys over there will rearrange that pretty face. We don't care who your daddy is. Got it? Are we clear?"

I was being threatened. Interesting. That didn't happen to me. This was a first. I felt very normal. I said what came naturally.

"I'm engaged."

Larissa didn't look convinced. "Don't hurt her," she repeated, before walking back over, to continue working her shaker.

"She works for my fiancé. I didn't come looking for her. That was seven years ago."

Larissa paused, her icy green eyes, lifting to meet mine in space. "Your reasons and excuses mean nothing. That girl is special. We all love her. We'll protect her at any and all cost. She didn't have a normal teenage life, those years robbed by that damn disease. You were the last real memory she had before it all went to shit. She's strong in many ways but her heart is innocent, fragile and please don't forget that."

"I realize that, but I'm not going to date her, it isn't like I can hurt her."

Larissa rolled her eyes and muttered a curse. "You're the only one who can dumbass. Didn't you hear what I said?"

I started to say more when Larissa's eyes lifted to someone behind me. I turned to see Bliss dancing closely against Micha. They were looking in each other's eyes talking. "She looks like she has her eyes on someone else."

Larissa laughed. "Micah? Not in this lifetime."

That answered my question about them. The relief that came from her words was the only warning I needed. She was right. If I didn't control my fucking emotions Bliss could get hurt and it would be on me. As much as I was tempted and drawn to her, Bliss York wasn't in my future, though she was firmly set in my past.

Chapter Eleven

♥ BLISS YORK ♥

"**W**HO IS HE Bliss?" Micah asked the moment we started dancing. He was staring at Nate over my shoulder. Trying to figure out how he knew him. "He's from my past. But his fiancé doesn't know and she's my boss. It's best the past stay passed. Please don't say anything. I don't want any further discussion."

Micah scowled and turned his eyes to mine. "He's the guy from that summer."

I imagine most people don't have their first love or relationship remembered as having been so important and vital by EVERYONE around them. Nate was "the guy" because he was the only real one I had when I was a teen before it all came crashing down. My sickness came soon after Nate and permanently changed my life. He was B.C. and would forever remain B.C., innocently cast into that roll. Nate was remembered for having played it. Being there before my diagnosis.

It was only a matter of time before they all knew who he was. Which meant this dance had to be short and was getting shorter every second. When I'd invited Octavia to come here tonight all

I'd been thinking about was forcing myself to be around them and getting accustomed to that. I didn't think she would come. This wasn't her kind of place. She didn't "slum" with the locals and whatnot.

Until I saw them walk in the door I didn't think my friends would remember Nate. It hadn't even crossed my mind.

"Are you okay? I mean with him being here? And engaged?"

As if there was an answer to that. A normal person would be fine. It was seven years ago. I should be completely okay with it. That was what made sense.

"Yes, of course. It was another lifetime ago," I replied.

"B.C."

"Exactly."

The song finished. I had to move. "I need to get back in case someone else remembers who he is. Otherwise it will be like lightning striking in a big dry forest. When it catches one, the rest will catch to, and then the forest will burn."

"Very good analogy Bliss. He's talking to Larissa. She looks pissed off. I guess she remembered him. There's tree number two a burnin'."

Crap!

I hurried over to the bar just as Nate was turning around to leave. I quickly scanned his face for any sign of anger. I only saw mild frustration. Glancing at Larissa behind him I noticed her scowling at his back. Yep, okay, she remembered him. Alright, here we go. Trees just a burnin' and a burnin'.

"Do I need to be concerned that anyone else may recall who I am and want to kill me?" He asked and smiled disgustedly.

"I think Micah will help if they start to. I'll be back at the table in a minute. I need to get a drink."

"Why did you invite her, hell, us, into this, knowing what would happen?"

Good question.

"I'm not sure. Trust me I'm regretting it. Bad idea. Really bad idea."

Nate started to say something else and then stopped before he walked off.

I turned my attention to Larissa who was eagerly waiting for me. She knew I was here to talk to her. I rarely drank that much.

She asked "why can't the fiancé know you once had a thing?" Her expression spoke volumes, said she was annoyed, and so I answered bluntly and directly.

"Because he didn't tell her right away and now he thinks it will cause an issue. I like my job. I don't want to lose it."

Larissa rolled her eyes. "This isn't fucking junior high. He needs to be a man and get that shit out, air his clean and dirty laundry. He should tell the damn truth and be done with it."

"It's fine. I think it'll be better with her not knowing. Forgetting it ever happened works for me."

Larissa leaned forward, as close as she could get, resting her arms on the bar. "Does it really? It works for you? Or does it work for him?"

She thought I was protecting Nate. That's why she was pissed.

"Octavia is spoiled and thinks she's entitled. She's been a good boss, but if she thought I was a threat, she'd get rid of me in an instant. I need the job and the income and without any experience she gave me the chance I needed. I don't want to lose that. Even if I have to hide a secret."

"Bliss, you're making a mistake. He still has a thing for you. It's in his eyes. I'm never wrong about that. But he's not man enough to admit it. Don't forget that. Don't ever settle. You deserve a fairytale more than anyone I know. What you went through was tremendous. Devastating, and you have to have the best."

Because I was sick? What I went through was "tremendous"

and I "have to have the best?" These were words, part of the collection, I was used to hearing. But there was one always left unspoken. The "big word" never added to their comments. It hung silently in the balance. They all assumed because of it I should have the best. After CANCER it was supposed to be easy? No, nothing was. I still had to live this life and it was still going to be hard. Just like it was for everyone else.

"Thanks," was all I could say. If I said what I really felt about that I'd sound like a brat and have to stand there, arguing back and forth. So, I walked away with a smile on my face I didn't feel, but had already perfected, a long time ago when I was sick. My "false grin" was one of the best. I should win an Academy Award.

"Bliss!" Saffron's voice carried above the crowd and I cringed. She was already drinking and drunk. I could hear it in her slur. Where did she find all these people who would give her alcohol?

"And she's here. I've already texted Holland. There she comes," Crimson said, pointing to the door where Holland was walking in. She was dressed normally. Like she had been at home comfortably reading. Which I was sure she had been.

"But James is here! I came to see James!" Saffron giggled, her boobs almost falling from her top, which by the way was the size of a napkin.

Holland paused. The hurt in her eyes was quickly masked. She definitely had a thing for James.

"I'll take her outside," James said. He put his arm around her bare waist as Saffron beamed up at him, leaning into his body, loving the man like a puppy. "You're here," she cooed. "Jamesy is here with me."

"Yeah, but you already knew that," was his response.

"I was hoping he'd stay at the table and leave this alone. Why are guys so dumb?" Crimson replied disgusted

I didn't know the answer to this question. But I was wondering the same myself. Surely James knew what he was doing? How could he miss the look in Holland's eyes whenever she looked at him? Saffron was identical to her, but Holland didn't dress like Saffron and she was quieter, more withdrawn.

Was that what men wanted? The drawers of attention like Saffron? Damaged goods with expiration dates? I focused on the group at the table. Nate's arms were around Octavia's waist. They were talking and laughing, Jimmy being entertaining, because when he wanted he could be that. Nate seemed happy. Content.

My heart cracked a little more and weakened. I'd asked for this by inviting them. It was time I accepted it and learned to live with it.

~Nate Finlay~

IT HAD BEEN quiet last night on the way back to Octavia's house. When we walked inside she went to her room and closed the door. No words. Nothing.

There was no question as to what was wrong. I knew. It would take a complete idiot not to know what was up her ass. Hell, I knew this was going to be an issue while I was doing it. But fuck me if I hadn't been able to stop myself.

Bliss was hard not to watch. I tried. God, I so fucking tried. I did everything I could to keep from looking at her last night. But I was a man and Bliss . . . well Bliss was Bliss. She was hard to ignore. For me she was damn near impossible to ignore.

Finally, I had just given in and watched her. Let my eyes follow her every move. Knowing all along Octavia would notice and a fight would follow. Not because she was a jealous person. She wasn't. She didn't have time to focus on anyone other than herself. Very little room for jealousy.

No, Octavia was pissed because my looking at Bliss had been a slap in the face to her. Others saw it. Knew she wasn't my center of attention and that she couldn't deal with. I was fairly certain she was just going to take this out on me. Not Bliss.

However, I wasn't about to test that theory. When I woke up to find Octavia's bedroom already empty I hurried my ass up and got to her store. Bliss wouldn't be there for another hour so I had time to fix this shit if she in fact was going to let Bliss go because of me.

Walking into the office that Octavia had me set up for her in the back I could smell the expensive French perfume she loved to wear. It was appealing. One of the first things that got my attention when we met. I liked things to smell good and Octavia always smelled amazing. Money could do that for you.

She shot an annoyed glare my way before going back to whatever she was doing on her computer. "You're a bastard," she said with a hiss in her voice.

"I'm sorry."

I learned from my father that apologizing to a woman was easier than arguing with one. Sometimes this worked and sometimes it didn't. I was hoping this was one of those times that it worked. The frown in her brow however told me I was fucked. This wasn't going to be that easy.

"In front of all those people. Never, Nate Finlay, never have you humiliated me that way. If you had, we wouldn't be engaged and living together right now. I'd be done with you."

This was dramatic. Not her usual response to things.

"I was trying to figure her out. You're planning on leaving her here alone to run the place in a little over a month."

Octavia shot her heated gaze up from the screen and leveled me with it. "Don't fucking patronize me. She's beautiful and has that innocent farm girl thing. You couldn't take your eyes off her. It was obvious to everyone. Including her and she's as naïve as a female her age can be. Don't act like you did that for me."

Okay so maybe I should have gone with a different angle. But damn I didn't have one. Not really. I wanted to look at her last night and I had given up trying to pretend I wasn't drawn to her. Fascinated with her. Fuck it to hell. This was not the shit I wanted to deal with. This was not easy. I wanted easy.

"No woman her age that looks like that can be that naïve. I didn't trust it. I studied how her friends treated her and how she handled herself. You thinking she's trustworthy because she's some farm girl from Alabama is fucking naïve if you ask me."

Had I even sounded believable just now?

Octavia frowned. Like she was thinking about what I'd said as if it made sense. Surely she saw through my bullshit.

"You think I'm being too trustworthy?"

No. Not one damn bit. Bliss was as trustworthy as Octavia was ever going to get in an employee but this seemed to be working so I went with it. Anything to get Octavia over her snit and save Bliss's job.

"I did. Yes. But you're right. The girl is everything she appears. A bit immature for her age but she's middle class and needs a job. She seems willing to prove herself and the people close to her really like her. They trust her. And she didn't once meet my gaze last night. She didn't try to flirt or even give me a smile."

Octavia nodded slowly. "I noticed that. She had to see you watching her but she didn't take advantage of it. She ignored you completely. I respect that. We need to tell her though the truth. That you had been measuring her up. Testing her. She doesn't need to think you have any interest in her. She's not like us. She doesn't need to think she could fit into your world and mess up the best opportunity she's going to get in this town. God knows women can be stupid when it comes to you."

Most of what she had just said pissed me off.

Scratch that.

All of what she had just said pissed me off. I hated the elitist way Octavia's mind worked. It was the one thing I was afraid I wouldn't be able to live with the rest of my life. Or any part of my life. Bliss wasn't less than us because she had grown up differently. My own mother grew up very similar to Bliss and she was one of the smartest women I knew. That meant nothing.

There were some fucking idiots that had grown up at the country club with me. Money didn't make you important. It wasn't a one way ticket into the world of the elite. Especially for people like me and Octavia. We weren't rich. Our parents were. We were trust fund kids. Not exactly impressive.

But Bliss's job was at stake and I knew I had to play the role. Keep my thoughts to myself. Pretend I agreed. I could question this all later. When I wasn't standing here in front of a woman that was watching my every expression.

"Bliss isn't like us. You're right. She's a farm girl from Alabama with an inferior education and very little sense of the real world. She lives in a bubble here in Sea Breeze. One she won't ever get out of or hope to break free from. But that makes her safe. She's a good employee and one we now know you can trust."

Just saying all of that bullshit made me hate myself. It wasn't true. Bliss had beat a disease that took lives daily. If she wanted out of this damn town she'd get out. She'd create herself. She would achieve any goal she set for herself. She would fight until she had it. I believed that.

Octavia nodded. "Good. I'm glad you agree." She then let out a laugh. "The idea of her ever fitting into your world is ludicrous anyway. I guess I was tired last night. Being too sensitive. I should have known you weren't interested in someone like her. I've never known you to settle for someone so beneath you."

Chapter Twelve

♥ BLISS YORK ♥

"**B**LISS ISN'T LIKE us . . . She's a farm girl from Alabama with an inferior education and very little sense of the real world. She lives in a bubble here in Sea Breeze. One she won't ever get out of or hope to break free from . . ."

Those words ran through my head over and over again. Long after I had walked away from Octavia's office door. I'd needed to confirm a price on sandals she had ordered. That was it. Nothing more.

Yet . . . I'd been crushed instead. A pair of the sandals were still in my hand as I stood in the store front and stared blankly out the window. *Farm girl from Alabama.* I winced and closed my eyes tightly wishing I could erase that. If only I had waited a few more minutes before walking back there. I'd still be living in my happy bubble where Nate had watched me all evening and my heart had soared with hope.

This was my punishment. I shouldn't have wanted him to watch me. To look at me. Because he wasn't free. I had wanted to take Octavia's fiancé away. That was wrong. This was what I deserved. The pain of knowing Nate's real feelings about me.

He wasn't the same boy from that summer. He was grown and he had changed. More so than me. I was stronger. Less naïve. The real world and its horror had touched me briefly. But the pain of heartbreak was new. I preferred not knowing how this felt.

I had been sheltered from so much. How the world saw me was one of those things I didn't really know. Until now. I liked to think I was on the road to making a real life for myself. That my beating leukemia had made me strong. I wasn't easily beaten down and I had goals. A lot of goals. When people saw me I hoped they also saw all of that.

Apparently, they didn't. I was a farm girl, with an inferior education and no sense of the real world. It was a slap in the face and a knife to the chest. If only these damn shoes had a price on them I could still be in a happy place.

"Oh good you're here. We need to add something to the window. A flash. A touch of what the others don't have. White twinkle lights or the feel of Manhattan. Give the shoppers a taste of what they're getting when they walk through those doors. Draw them in. The clothing isn't enough."

I still had a job to do. More so than before I had something to prove too. This farm girl from Alabama could impress them. I wasn't an idiot. The pressure to do so however made me somewhat nervous. What if I gave her ideas and he shot them down? What if my ideas were simple? Just like Nate said I was.

"Don't get me wrong. You've done a beautiful job displaying the best of what we offer. Kudos to you for that. Now we need to take it a step further. Give them what they don't get when they look in the other windows. Show them why this store stands out. Why they can't walk past it. Why they must buy something from Octavia's."

Nate had walked in while she was going on about making the window stand out. Ignoring him before had been difficult. But now . . . it was easier. I had something to prove but not to him. I had to prove it to myself. Remind myself I wasn't what he said I was. That all he saw was what he assumed. There was more to me than that and he'd never get the privilege of knowing. Our past was now firmly that. The door was closed. Memories shoved so far back it would take a shovel and days of work to dig them out. I was done with all there was to do with Nate Finlay.

I had to show Bliss York that she was strong, smart, and capable of reaching her goals. All of them and more. Nate's presence faded to the background and I turned my complete and full attention to the window display. My focus was centered on that and only that.

One thing they didn't know about a girl from Alabama was when we were backed into a corner we came out with both fists up and a will to win.

"I like the twinkle lights. This is a coastal town and people shopping here will be looking for something that reminds them they're enjoying the sand, surf, and sun. The twinkle lights can be the sunlight, let's bring in sand for the floor but then the sea breeze can't be seen. We need something that draws the eye. White feathers suspended as if flying free in the wind surrounding the display would be unique and attention grabbing."

I wasn't sure where the idea came from. I just opened my mouth and let the ideas fly. Not caring how ridiculous it may sound. The picture began taking shape in my head and I added to it and didn't stop talking for Octavia to say anything until I had it all outlined. Shown her where it all would go and then explained why it would sell. One would think I'd worked at retail stores my entire life the way I was blabbing on about what the shoppers wanted.

When I was finally done, I waited for her reaction. Prepared for the worst but knowing I hadn't backed down due to fear or the fact Nate had given me a major blow to my self-esteem only minutes before.

"It's brilliant," were the words out of her mouth. I let out the breath I had been holding. I agreed with her. I wasn't sure how I created it so quickly and relayed it so clearly but I had. And I was thankful I had. This had been a moment I needed to show myself, not them, that I could do this.

"The sand and feathers. It'll be the most talked about store front in town. We need to order the perfect twinkle lights. Hang them straight down from ceiling to floor like you said. Nate, Google lights and see what you find. I'm going to make a call about getting some sand. Bliss you find the feathers. Large white perfect feathers won't be easy to find."

I nodded and reached into my pocket for my phone. I didn't watch as Octavia left through the backdoor to see if Nate followed. I Googled feathers and began my search. His presence was there. I could feel his gaze on me, I just chose to ignore it. Turning my back to him I studied the window that we'd be transforming and wondered if we needed to add anything else. Maybe some silver. The white with silver would be striking.

"You knocked this out of the fucking park. Blew Octavia's mind."

Nate had come closer. His voice was deep and there was a touch of pride in his tone. I found that odd considering his words to Octavia about me only moments earlier.

"Getting the sand in will be a bitch but it's brilliant." He was trying to get me to respond. He wasn't used to me ignoring him. I wasn't a rude person. Kindness was something I always wanted to be sure I had plenty of. However today with Nate I wasn't feeling it. Turning around I shot him with a piercing glare.

"Us farm girls from Alabama can surprise even you I guess." I didn't wait for him to respond. Instead, I walked straight to the back where he wouldn't be able to say more or Octavia would hear him. He knew I'd heard. That was all that had to be said.

Nate and I had no past, present, or future as far as I was concerned.

Now, to find those feathers.

~NATE FINLAY~

MOTHERFUCKER.

Dammit to hell! Of all the things for Bliss to hear me say that was the absolute last thing I'd ever want her to hear. It was all bullshit. I was trying to save her job. To reassure Octavia and it backfired in my fucking face.

I had to go outside. To my truck. Away from it all. So, I could get control of my mouth. Because right now all I wanted to do was explain to Bliss why I'd said it and not give a damn if Octavia heard me. Which would hurt Bliss more. Not help.

But that look in her eyes was devastating. It said more than the unconcerned expression she was using to hide the pain. She hadn't been able to mask it. I'd wounded her bad.

I rubbed my hand over my chest to ease some of the ache there. I didn't want her to hurt. Fuck I didn't want to make her do anything but smile. She lit up a room when she smiled. Anyone who would extinguish that didn't deserve to breathe. Bliss was as close to perfect as a female got and what I'd done was killing me.

I stared at the closed door and weighed my options. I could go back in there and explain it to her. Fix this. Tell her exactly how I felt about her. How I was in awe of her. Or I could let her keep her job and go see her later.

Tonight.

After work. At her apartment.

That was what I'd do. Her place was safe. Octavia wouldn't see me there and she wouldn't know I'd talked to Bliss. She wouldn't know anything. I started for the door and stopped. I couldn't look at Bliss again and keep my mouth shut. I didn't want her to think I meant those words and if she flashed me those shining, pretty blue eyes, so full of hurt again I would crack and blurt it all out.

I went back to my truck and jerked the door open then climbed inside. I'd go somewhere else for the day. I could call Octavia and make up some excuse why I had to go. I wasn't her bitch and that store wasn't my responsibility. If I didn't want to work in it, I didn't have to.

Driving around I'd ignored three text from Octavia. Funny, when she didn't need me, she never texted. That suddenly annoyed me. I was thankful she didn't drive me nuts just two weeks ago.

Bliss had changed it all. She hadn't meant to but she had. Seeing her and being near her made me question just how happy I actually was with this life I had planned out. I'd caught myself thinking about how I missed drama in my life and for me that was crazy talk. For most men that was crazy talk.

Though Bliss wasn't dramatic. She would mean more. Need more. And I wasn't sure I could handle either. She deserved it all. After the shit she'd been through she deserved a prince and I wasn't one of those. I was more like the bad boy. The one you spend a little time with then move on along.

Octavia got that. She was okay with me and how I was. Somehow that didn't matter so much anymore. I pulled into Bliss's parking lot and picked up my phone. Octavia's three text were:

Where are you?

Can you get some storage shelves?

I've got to go for the day. Bliss is closing up. I'll see you tonight.

That was it. She didn't keep asking where I was. She didn't call me. She didn't seem to give a fuck. What man didn't want that? A stupid one.

I texted back:

"I thought I'd take a drive and go see Grandpop. See you tonight. "

That was all she would require. No more explanation. Nothing.

A simple "K" was Octavia's reply.

Easy. So damn easy. But was easy what I really wanted? Was it what anyone really wanted?

I walked from my parked truck to Bliss's condo and tried to think of how I would explain this. What I would say. How I would say it. Nothing sounded good enough. I was just going to wing it and apologize. Tell her the truth. Get that hurt look out of her eyes. God, that was hard to see.

When I stopped outside her door I could hear voices inside. More than just her and Eli. Several. Loud voices laughing and talking. Like they were having a party. I thought real hard about if I wanted to do this right now. Maybe I should wait. I'd wanted to get her alone. Not with a condo full of people.

Those eyes were haunting me though and I had to fix this. I knocked. The sound didn't lessen and I wondered if they'd even heard me. Should I knock louder? They needed a damn doorbell.

Before I could think too much about it the door swung open and Bliss was standing there. I saw people behind her but I couldn't focus on what was going on in the room. All I could see was her. She went from smiling to a frown immediately. Then there was a flash of anger in her eyes.

"I need to talk to you," I said before she could slam the door in my face. I wasn't sure if she would do that but in case I wasn't taking a chance.

"I heard enough," she replied curtly. Then, like her knight in shining armor, Eli was beside her. The scowl on his face said he knew. She'd told him. He wanted to bash my face in and I didn't blame him. Although he shouldn't try it, Eli wasn't a match for me.

"What you heard and what was really happening are two different things. Your job was on the line, Bliss. She thought I was attracted to you. I had to do something to fix it."

Her eyes widened and the frown faded.

"She's busy," Eli said before she could respond.

But she placed a hand on his arm. "No, I want to talk to him. I'll be back."

He looked ready to grab her and slam the door in my face. "Are you sure?"

She tilted her head back and looked up at him. "Yes."

With a sigh, he moved back then shot me one more warning glare.

Bliss stepped outside and closed the door behind her. I was glad Eli was on the other side and not opening his mouth. I didn't need his opinion nor did Bliss need protection from me.

"I'm listening," she said, crossing her arms over her chest. She was wearing a tank top and a pair of cutoff jeans. Her feet were bare and her toes were bright pink. She'd had more than one glass of wine tonight. I could smell it on her breath. All of that appealed to me. I wanted to get closer. Touch her. Inhale her scent. Damn, I was fucked up.

"You know I couldn't keep my eyes off you last night. You caught me looking at you more than once. So did Octavia. I had to tell her I was making sure you were safe. That she could trust you. I had to give her some excuse or she'd have fired you. Even though you are the best employee she's going to find. I didn't mean a word I said. It was all bullshit that she needed to hear. None of it was true. I . . ."

"I quit." She interrupted me.

I paused and made sure I had just heard her correctly. She quit? And Octavia hadn't told me?

"What? When?"

She reached up and tucked a strand of hair behind her ear. Even her ear was perfect. Or maybe I was so biased I thought everything about her was perfect.

"I told her just before I left for the day. I thanked her for the job then told her I overheard the two of you, and that I didn't want to work for anyone who thought so poorly of me. She didn't even apologize. I don't think she even cared."

Octavia wouldn't. Fuck if that didn't piss me off too.

"You needed that job."

She gave me an affirmative nod. "Yes I did. But until I can find another one I will be working as a waitress at Live Bay. Serving drinks."

And I wouldn't see her anymore. Unless I was at Live Bay when she was working. The day to day of knowing that she was at Octavia's was gone just like that. The ache formerly in my chest was now a hollow spot. Empty. And I did what any desperate man would do.

I grabbed her waist, pulled her against me, and kissed her until neither of us could breathe.

Chapter Thirteen

❤ BLISS YORK ❤

I WAS LOST for a moment. What was right and what was wrong didn't register in my brain. Not then. My mind and heart were both drenched in this kiss and I let it happen. I didn't just let it happen I held on for dear life and then some. My hands grabbed at his muscular arms as my body pressed against his. I could stay like this forever, his frame moving against mine, and the taste of his mouth forcing my toes to curl.

What he'd said and how much it had hurt didn't matter. I believed him. He hadn't meant it. The Nate I knew wasn't cruel and elitist. It had been a ploy to save my job. A job, after overhearing them, I didn't want. And I admit this was better than my memory. But, of course, he was now a man. And he knew exactly what to do and how to do it.

No I didn't care about anything else. This was everything.

Running my hands up his arms I inhaled his scent and I felt like moaning with pleasure. For a virgin with very little experience my body was buzzing and I ached to get closer. To have more.

Just as my hands found his broad shoulders and his hands found my bottom I remembered what did matter. The one thing that made this wrong. It was like ripping off my arm or stepping back from the sun into the cold shadows. But I did it. I broke the kiss and used both my hands to shove him back. Away from me. Away from what I wanted but couldn't have.

This wasn't okay. He wasn't free. He belonged to someone else.

"Bliss," he began, and I shook my head no. He didn't need to say anything.

"That was wrong," I told him. He already knew it and maybe that had been what he was going to say. But I needed to be the one to say it. Hearing him confess that this kiss had been a mistake wasn't something I could handle at the moment. My heart was taking a serious beating because reality had suddenly set in.

"Nothing about that was wrong," he argued, taking a step toward me. I took a step back.

"Stop. Don't. Yes, it was," I said. Although I didn't agree with him, those words soothed me as much as they pained me. He wasn't saying he'd made a mistake. I was thankful for that, even if it was selfish.

"Bliss, look at me," he pleaded. I didn't think that was a good idea. If I saw those eyes and those lips of his I wasn't sure I wouldn't throw myself at him. He wasn't mine to touch. To enjoy. He wasn't mine to laugh with and kiss. He wasn't mine to hold. He was someone else's and I'd kissed him.

The worst thing about it was I didn't regret it. I should feel ashamed. Terrible. I was an awful human being but I did not care. I wouldn't give that kiss up for anything. I'd just live with my crime. My character flaw. Who was I kidding, I had a lot of flaws, but now I knew I had a really major defect. I'd become "the other woman."

"You should go," I said, still looking down.

He sighed and I heard him let out a frustrated growl. "I can't, this isn't . . . fuck!" He wasn't making complete thoughts but I understood every word. I felt it too. Even the curse word at the end. "There's something there. Something between us. Always has been, since the first time I saw you. But that something is scary as hell. What I have now . . . it's easy." His last word trailed off like he had admitted something he was ashamed of.

My heart was already broken but it was shattering as we stood there. We did have something. A connection that drew me to him. Made me want to be close to him. He made my world brighter. I'd thought that was because of my limited experience with guys but he felt it too. It wasn't just me.

That didn't change anything though. He wanted easy. I wasn't easy. Was it because I had been sick? I wasn't sick anymore. Again, with people seeing me as the sick girl. I hated that. I didn't want to be labeled that by anyone especially Nate.

"I'm not sick . . . I am clear of any cancer," I said the words lifting my eyes to meet his. "I have been for almost four years. "

He frowned and studied me a moment. Like he didn't understand anything I'd just said.

The door behind me opened. I turned to see Eli. "You good?"

He was worried. We'd been out here longer than I expected. Eli had probably been pacing in front of the door waiting on me to return. He was good like that. He hadn't once treated me like the sick girl. Even when I had no hair and spent my days too sick to keep down food.

"We're fine," I assured him.

He didn't look convinced but he waited a second then reluctantly closed the door. He'd want a complete recap of this and I wouldn't be able to give it to him. I couldn't tell him I'd kissed another woman's fiancé. Because he'd expect me to feel remorse. Admit my fault. And I couldn't. If it was anyone else, I would, but not Nate. First, he'd been mine, not Octavia's.

"I know you're clear of cancer. Why are you telling me that now?"

Because he said I wasn't easy. He wanted easy. Didn't he remember what he had said? "You said I was scary and you wanted easy."

His eyes looked sad as my words sank in. Then he took a step toward me and I didn't move back this time. I was deciding I might not care about the fact he wasn't free. I was a hussy. Or at least becoming one.

"That's not what I meant," he replied. "My life . . . the way I feel for you is intense. It'll never be easy."

"So you want to feel what?"

"Free. Without attachment."

He wanted to feel nothing. He didn't want to chance the pain to experience the great. He was a coward. He didn't love Octavia. He loved how simple it was with her. She was never around and she didn't seem to want to talk to him much. That wasn't a relationship. That wasn't what my parents had. And I wanted what they had. Every girl dreamed of that kind of devotion.

"Then there's nothing left to say," I replied.

I should have turned and went back inside then. Left him without saying anything more. Made a grand exit. But I stood there. Because I knew once I walked away that was it. I may never see him again and I just couldn't let him go yet.

"I'm sorry," were his choice words.

"Me too, Nate Finlay." Then I forced my feet to move, my heart to let go and my brain to shut up. Getting inside was vital. I didn't trust my mouth not to blurt out something I'd regret. Something stupid, like begging him to love me. To just try. That was something he should want to do. Not something I should have to beg for. My mother was the center of my father's world. They loved us kids but we knew they adored each other. It gave us security and also showed us what the "real thing" was supposed to look like.

One day I'd find a man to love me that way. As much as my heart wished it were Nate, I knew it wasn't. And that was going to hurt for a very long time.

~NATE FINLAY~

I WAS GOING to end up drinking myself into an early grave. They'd find me dead on the side of the road. Or maybe my liver would fail. Heck, I was in Alabama. There was a good chance I'd say the wrong thing to some guy and he'd blow the top of my head off. Fuck, if I cared.

With that thought, I took another swig from the bottle of Maker's Mark in my hand. Currently, this was how I dealt with life. When I was sober, I thought about Bliss. Who was I kidding? I was hammered and thought about Bliss. It just hurt less with the numbness the alcohol delivered.

Octavia hadn't said much about Bliss quitting. Her response when I asked her the next day was "oh, she quit. I'll replace her soon enough." She hadn't even given me the reason. I fucking knew the reason, but the fact Octavia was keeping it from me pissed me off.

But then everything about Octavia was beginning to piss me off. I was in a state of constant annoyance.

I took another drink. I was parked outside Live Bay. I thought about going inside but figured this bottle and my truck would do just fine for the moment. I didn't need a crowd to witness this level of low.

When Octavia had left today after hiring some thirty-year-old soccer mom who didn't have a clue what was going on, I figured I could either go back to Rosemary Beach or I could drink. I chose the drink.

Simply because leaving Sea Breeze meant leaving Bliss. And although I hadn't seen her in five days the idea of being that far away from her was like a sharp pain in my chest. Which was also a reason to drink. So drink I did.

Leaning back in my seat I watched the people going inside laughing and having a damn ole good time. They weren't like me. They were here because it was fun. This was a jolly fucking good time. I held out my bottle and said a cheers to the idiots outside. They couldn't see me through the tint in my windows and the darkness outside but I did it anyway. Made me feel less alone.

Why was I engaged? I didn't want to be married. Hell, I was too fucking young to be married. What was my problem? Had I been desperate to get out of Rosemary that I thought marriage was the answer? Jesus at some point I'd lost my mind.

I wanted easy and Octavia was easy? Hell no! There was no easy relationships. Marriage was the hardest of them all. Why in God's name had I thought that was a good idea?

Picking up my phone I texted her just that:

Why the fuck are we engaged? I don't want to be married. And damned if you do. We don't fit.

I paused and took another drink before I pressed send. Because this was it. I was telling the truth and with that came a consequence. I was ending it with Octavia. Pressing send was the end. She wasn't dramatic and she wouldn't beg me to stay. She'd take that as doubt and she'd walk away. Easy. So fucking easy.

I pressed send.

Staring at the doors to Live Bay I wondered if Bliss was in there. Was she why I'd just pressed send? Would this make a difference in my decision about her? She wasn't easy. That hadn't changed. And I didn't want marriage. Possibly ever. She would.

My phone didn't vibrate a response. There was no sudden argument from Octavia. She didn't have an answer for me either. She said nothing. I drank two thirds of the bottle before I finally decided maybe I should go inside. See Bliss. Because she was why I was sitting here hammered off my ass after all.

It took me three tries before I could find the door knob. Even then I couldn't manage to open it. Sighing, I closed my eyes and laid my head back. Fuck this. I couldn't drive if I couldn't open the damn door. So I'd do what? Sleep here all night? Shit. Just what I wanted Bliss to see if she was here. Me passed out in my truck.

A knock on the door startled me and I turned my head to see Eli fucking Hardy standing there. He was in his polo shirt and his perfectly styled hair. There was that judgmental frown on his face that made you just want to punch him in the nose. Or maybe it just made me want to punch him in the nose. Bliss didn't seem to want to hurt him because he was tidy and clean.

But hell what a bore that was. He had to bore her to death. He bored me by just looking at him. I wanted to close my eyes and go back to passing out. But he knocked again and I knew he wasn't going to leave me alone.

I tried again to open the door and after a few attempts finally managed it. Mr. Perfect's frown was even deeper by the time I got it open and that made me want to slam the door back. I would if I could figure out how to . . .

"You smell like whisky," were his oh so wise words.

"No shit," I drawled. He was a fucking Einstein.

"Why are you here? Bliss gets off work in a few minutes and this isn't something he needs to see."

Well ain't he thoughtful. Worried about Bliss seeing me drunk. Why? Had she never seen a drunk man before? I figured she had seeing as she was working at a damn club. I doubted she would be too shocked by what I was doing.

"She would be," he replied angrily.

"Huh?" Had he just read my thoughts?

Eli shook his head. "Move over. I'm driving you home."

The hell he was. I managed a laugh then. A loud one. Eli Hardy thought he was going to save me? I laughed harder.

"She will be out here any minute. You're drunk and being a complete dick. She doesn't need to see this. You've hurt her enough."

Wait . . . what? I hadn't hurt her. I was gentle with her. Explained myself. I had fucking destroyed me apparently but I'd been good to her. I didn't want to hurt her.

Eli was staring at me. What was his problem?

"She needs to move on," he once again replied as if he knew what I was thinking. Weird shit.

"I'm sleeping here. She won't see me," I argued.

"Your truck is parked right here. How will she miss it?"

Good point. "Well she won't know I'm in it. You can't see me in the dark."

"I saw you," he shot back. "Now move over. I'm taking you home."

I wasn't going to Octavia's. I was pretty damn sure I'd just broken it off with her or had I dreamed that? Maybe I should text her again to be sure.

"What is your problem? Do you not care that you're hurting her?"

There he was with the hurting again. I hadn't hurt her. "I'm not hurting her."

He was the one to laugh this time but he didn't laugh like he meant it. Instead he sounded hard and cold. Like he was the one annoyed. Hell what did he have to be annoyed with. This was my fucking truck he was invading.

"Eli? Nate?" there was her voice. I'd dreamed about that voice.

"Bliss," I said wanting Eli to move so I could see her. I missed her.

"I got this. You go on home," Eli said not moving.

"You got what?" she asked and I started to say something when she moved in front of him moving him back away from the door with her small body.

"Oh God. You stink of whisky. Are you okay?"

I was now. If she'd climb up in this truck I'd be more than okay. "Just drunk sweetheart. Not anything serious."

She looked concerned. "I'm driving you home. Eli you follow us so you can give me a ride home."

"No, I'll drive him," Eli offered.

"He doesn't want you to. I'll drive him."

"No, Bliss."

"Eli, stop. You don't get to make decisions for me."

I wanted to agree with that but I had a hard time keeping my eyes open.

"Do you even know where he is staying? He's wasted. He can't remember shit."

"I know Octavia's house. I worked for her remember."

That was when I needed to find my words and open my damn eyes. I couldn't go there. Not now.

"I think, no, I'm positive, I think I'm positive. Fuck if I can remember but I am pretty damn sure that I broke up with her. Can't go to her house."

"What?" That was Bliss and I wanted to focus on her face. She was blurry though. It wasn't easy. I'd missed that face. That smile. Those eyes. And when it is put right in front of me I can't even focus on it. Fucking shame.

"What? Oh, yeah, I don't want to be married."

There as silence then.

"He can go to his grandfather's." That was Eli.

"No. Not like this. We will take him to our place."

"What?" Eli's tone almost made me laugh.

"Don't be difficult. He's almost passed out. Just let me take him to our place. He can sleep it off on the sofa and figure things out in the morning. He's obviously upset."

I kept my eyes closed because this was sounding better and better.

"He hurt you, Bliss."

She didn't reply right away and I wanted to ask her about that. See if he was right. I didn't mean to hurt her. I'd never want that.

"I know. But he needs me. That's all that matters right now."

My chest felt warm and tight. If I could I'd find a way to make this all right. But at the moment the darkness clawing at me won out and the world went quiet. There were no more voices to hear.

Chapter Fourteen

♥ BLISS YORK ♥

ELI WAS FURIOUS. Okay maybe that was an exaggeration. Eli was mad at me. That was the truth. I'd driven Nate back to our place last night and managed to get him to walk from the truck to the sofa in our living room. He'd said a lot of things I knew were drunken ramblings but they'd been nice. They'd been so nice I had stayed up most of the night thinking about them.

Should I have brought him back here? Probably not. Eli was right. I was asking to get hurt some more. But I wasn't able to leave him or take him to his grandfather's place, which would have made sense. I wanted him here, where I could watch him sleep. I was now venturing on creepy. Great.

The things Nate Finlay made me do. If he had any idea how I felt about him this would be humiliating. But I felt like I had kept my real feelings disguised enough. Being in love with a boy from seven years ago was embarrassing. He had moved on. I hadn't. My life had been paused. But I hadn't forgotten him.

Last night Eli was upset. He had gone in his room and slammed the door. I fought the urge to go talk to him. Ask him to understand and not be mad. That was what I would normally do. At least I think that was what I'd normally do. Eli had never been angry with me before. This was all very new.

Now I had a guy passed out drunk on my sofa and my best friend was angry with me. These were normal occurrences for a girl my age. It was time I lived a little. Felt the pains of growing up. Finding my way in this world.

That sounded extremely dramatic. I definitely didn't sound easy. And Nate wanted easy. Except last night he'd said he had broken up with Octavia. I wasn't sure I believed him since he was so hammered he had passed out. But then he had drank almost a fifth of whisky.

I curled my feet under me and took a sip of the coffee I had made. He'd be waking up soon. At least I hoped he would. It might be best if he was gone before Eli woke up. I had brought him here but what had I wished to accomplish. It wasn't like this would be different. He had said he didn't want me less than a week ago. I doubted that had changed.

Just because he had called me "beautiful" and "the most perfect girl" he'd ever seen didn't mean much. He'd also said he missed watching Teenage Mutant Ninja Turtles. Alcohol made him very sappy.

I think last night he was just missing the past. All of it. I was just a part of his past. But the past was just that. The simplicity of childhood was gone. I missed it too. I missed him. But that boy was gone. Replaced with a man I didn't know. Not really.

A groan came from the sofa and I watched as he stretched. At least he was going to wake up before Eli got out of bed. My thoughts halted then and I was distracted by the way his tanned muscular arms flexed as he moved them and yawned. I watched a wince touch his face and I figured that was the morning after alcohol pain.

Nate really was incredibly sexy. His body, his face, the way he moved. Even last night when he had been staggering drunk I'd wanted him. He had that appeal that was impossible to ignore.

"Fuck," he groaned covering his face with his hand and rubbing hard as if trying to wash away his memories of last night. Or the pounding headache he was sure to have. I had never been drunk but I had seen plenty people drink too much then pay for it the next day.

"I have an aspirin and some water when you're ready for it. Then a cup of black coffee might help." I told him and he froze.

I smiled into my cup. He had forgotten where he was. This was kind of fun. Even if I wouldn't see him again it was fun having Nate here.

Slowly he turned his head until he was looking at me. His half lidded eyes were bloodshot. He couldn't quite get them open. I watched as he winced again, the sunlight streaming through the window finding his face and neck.

"That wasn't a dream. Shit," he mumbled then threw his arm over his eyes. "Why did you bring me here?"

His voice was raspy and deep. I wondered if he always sounded that way when he woke up in the mornings. I liked it. Who wouldn't like it? That was the kind of thing that made your mind think of other things it shouldn't.

"You said you couldn't go to Octavia's." I told him. Had to say something. His grandfather was technically in this building, but I didn't point that out.

"You should have left me there in my truck. It's what I deserved."

"Security at Live Bay would have called the cops and you'd have ended up going to jail for the night to sleep it off."

He lifted his arm some to peek at me. "So you brought me here. To your place. When my grandfather is in the same building."

I shrugged. "Wasn't sure which condo and you weren't really

up for talking or directions last night."

He let out a moan and moved to sit up. The covers fell from his chest and it was bare. When had he taken off his shirt? I hadn't done that but I wasn't complaining. His chest was magazine cover ready. What woman wouldn't want to see that?

"Give it to me straight. What did I say?" he was concerned and I figured he remembered enough to be concerned. I'd leave the part out where he said if he married it would "be to me." Or that he thought about me "every damn minute of the day" so much "it crowded his thoughts." These were drunken outbursts I didn't believe and he'd want to make sure I didn't. That would be too painful. I would hold onto that forever.

"You broke up with Octavia or at least you think you did." That needed some clarification.

"Shit. I mean, I'm glad, but shit. I have to call her and talk this out. No telling what my text said. I'm scared to even look." He patted his pockets. "Where's my phone?"

"You dropped it in your truck. I left it in there."

He nodded then rubbed his face roughly. "Where's Eli?"

Eli was probably in his room listening and pissed off still. "Asleep."

Nate stood up. "I should go."

That was it? He wasn't going to talk about anything? Nothing he said? Nothing? He wasn't engaged anymore. But he didn't seem very interested in me either. Instead he looked like he wanted to bolt and couldn't get out of here quick enough.

"Okay. Your keys are on the bar," I told him and didn't move to get up and give them to him. I was still reeling over the fact he was just going to leave. We weren't going to talk. Nothing.

When had I missed the fact Nate Finlay had become an asshole?

He paused and I waited sipping my coffee and staring straight ahead out the window. I didn't know what to say or how to deal with this. It was like an awkward walk of shame but there had been no sex. No one night stand.

"Thanks for bringing me here. Making sure I didn't end up sleeping it off behind bars. My parents would freak the hell out if I ended up in jail."

Was this the equivalent of "It was good. Thanks for the hot fuck."? Because it felt like it.

"Like I said, I couldn't leave you there."

He didn't move and I didn't look at him. I refused to let him see what I really felt at this moment. I guess he'd go find another "easy" to replace Octavia. Even though last night he had told me he didn't want easy anymore. He wanted more. That had been drunken crap too. Yet I'd thought about it all night long.

"Bliss, did I say something I need to answer for this morning?"

He didn't remember anything.

"No, nothing. Good luck," I replied sparing him one glance as I stood up.

He didn't move at first and I thought maybe he was going to push for more. But before I knew it he was walking to the door.

When it opened, I let myself look. To mark this in my memory. Nate Finlay walking away from me. I needed to get him out of my heart and my head.

Our eyes locked and neither of us said a word. I wondered if he could read my eyes because in his I saw things that couldn't be correct. The regret I saw was wishful thinking. He didn't regret this. He was walking away with ease. No concern. No questions. But I was the one hurting. I was always the one hurting.

"Thanks again," he said and all I could do was nod.

When the door closed behind him I let out a sigh and my shoulders fell. Eli stepped from his room and I couldn't look at him. He'd listened to it all. He knew I had brought Nate here hoping for something . . . something I couldn't even put a name to.

Eli's strong arms wrapped around me and I curled into him. But I didn't cry. I wasn't that weak. I never would be again.

~NATE FINLAY~

I SAT ON my Grandpop's sofa for three hours staring. At nothing really. My thoughts were on Bliss and this morning. They were also on my sudden single status. I'd decided to finally get serious with Octavia because I was tired of my relationships just being about sex. There was supposed to be more than sex and I knew that. But what I'd had with Octavia wasn't enough.

The simple text I had gotten from her said more than enough:

Glad you figured that out sooner rather than later.

That was it. Nothing else. No phone call or dramatic outburst. Just one text. So fucking easy. Or was it so fucking empty. Maybe empty meant easy.

I could sit here and wonder if I had just screwed up a good thing. But that was wasting my time. Because I was free and all I could think about was Bliss. I should go right back to her apartment and tell her I wanted her. I wanted us. I wanted a chance.

For some reason though I couldn't manage to do it. Maybe it was waking up in her apartment hung over and unsure exactly what I'd said to her the night before. Or hell I might be the world's dumbest asshole. Who the fuck knew. All I knew was sitting here was just all I could get myself to do.

Last night I'd wanted nothing more than to be free to have Bliss. Today I was free and I was scared. The urge to call my mom was strong but I fought it. I was a man and I didn't need my mother's advice. Besides she'd be so happy I'd broken it off with Octavia she'd have a hard time focusing on the Bliss problem.

A hard knock on the door tore me from my inner battle and I looked toward the door confused. Who the hell would be knocking? Grandpop was at work and anyone who knew him knew that's where they'd find him. I waited and another aggressive knock had my curiosity peaked.

I went to the door and opened it expecting to see someone there for Grandpop and finding Bliss instead.

"I have something to say," she announced and walked into the apartment brushing past me.

"Okay," I managed to reply watching her. She spun around with her hands on her hips as she glared at me angrily. She was pissed and she was hot as hell. She also knew where my grandpop's apartment was. She'd lied about that.

"I'm done. Don't come around me. Don't show up drunk where I work. Go back to Rosemary Beach and your country club friends and stay there. I will not let myself get hurt again by you. I've overcome too much to let some guy ruin my happy. Last night," she said then let out a laugh that didn't sound as if she thought it was funny at all. Her eyes were shinning with unshed tears. "I was so desperate for anything from you that I clung to the ramblings of a drunk man. I believed the nonsense that came out of your mouth and I thought maybe there was a chance. But I was wrong. Those were the silly hopes of the girl who once loved you. We're grown and we've both changed. I get it. But I want you gone. "

I didn't have time to respond before she stalked past me and out the door.

"Bliss, wait! What . . . what did I miss here?" I had just left her apartment this morning and she hadn't been so damn angry at me then.

She paused and I watched as her shoulders lifted then fell with an exaggerated sigh. Nothing was said for several moments.

I was about to say something else when finally she turned back to me. "I'm that girl," she said. "The girl who clings to the hopes a guy will notice her. A guy who she thinks about and daydreams about but he is just out of her reach. But I don't want to be that girl. Not anymore. I want to be the girl a guy will throw it all away for. A girl he fights for. I want to be worth it."

I was speechless as she then walked away. I watched her go until she turned the corner and was gone from sight. That wasn't easy. Not by a fucking long shot. I wasn't ready for her. To be the guy she wanted. I wasn't sure I'd ever be that guy for anyone.

She was right. I should go. Leave this place. Let her live her life and find that guy who deserved her. Me, I wasn't that guy. I wanted to be. But then I was terrified of it.

The hollow place in my chest ached at the thought of leaving here. It became a sharp pain when I thought of the guy who would end up loving her. The one she was looking for. Before I got in so deep I couldn't get out, I headed for my truck. I was going home. Back to Rosemary Beach. Bliss York wanted to find her fairytale and I wasn't going to stand in her way.

When I got to the parking lot she was there. Watching me. I almost turned and went back to my grandpops to save myself from this. I wanted Bliss to have it all. And I couldn't be that. I couldn't make promises to her. She meant too much.

"You're leaving."

She'd asked me to. Or more like ordered me to.

"Yeah."

She frowned. "It was that easy?"

I was confused now. "What?"

"To make you leave. It was that stinking easy."

"You did just tell me to leave." I reminded her.

"Yes. But deep down I thought you'd run after me and . . . and . . . I don't know. I just. Oh, never mind," she said with a wave of her hand as if she were tossing the idea away. "Don't go yet."

Women. Confusing as hell. "Why?"

"Because Nate Finlay I want one last night with you. If you're really leaving here then give me one night. Just one. That's all I'm asking."

Nothing about that sounded like a good idea. A night with Bliss would be tempting. She was too damn beautiful and distracting. I'd forget all the reasons why we couldn't work. "I don't think we should."

"You're right. We shouldn't. But I fought through chemo and lived. I survived and while I was sick and bald and scared do you know what I thought about to get me through?"

I shook my head because no I had no idea.

"You. Us. That summer. That memory was what I clung to. So, before you leave, I want it again. Something *like a memory* that I can have to pull out and remember."

Fuck.

The way my chest had just been ripped open I was having difficulty breathing. That wasn't what I expected. She'd thought of me . . . God knows I'd thought of her but I hadn't been facing death.

"Okay," I replied. This may be a bad idea but fuck me if I was going to tell her no now. Not after she just told me that.

"Thanks." That simple word so sincere. I wanted to go pull her in my arms and promise she'd always be safe. I'd make sure of it. But I couldn't because I had no way of knowing if she would. But if there was a God surely he'd give her a long life.

"I'll pick you up at seven," I told her.

Chapter Fifteen

I HAD A moment. You know those crazy moments where you run off and do something insane. Well I had that moment. I forced Nate Finlay to take me out on a date. What kind of desperate female even does that? It wasn't like I could back out now. I was stuck. I had acted like an idiot now I had to follow through and be done with it.

The next time I went out on a date it would be with someone who asked me because they wanted to. I was at least sticking to that. This thing tonight was a mistake. I knew it before it even started. Eli, not talking to me as he sat in front of the evening news eating a piece of grilled chicken and some steamed broccoli, agreed with that. He was not happy about this but he didn't get to make decisions for me. I got to make those and screw things up all by myself.

Deciding what to wear had been an all afternoon dilemma. I had tried on five dresses, two pants outfits and three with shorts and slides. Nothing was a winner but then did it really matter? It wasn't like tonight was going to be fun. It was going to be weird and awkward thanks to me.

I tried talking to Eli about this and he just stared at me blankly then turned his attention back to the television. He was disappointed in me. I could see it in his expression even if he tried to look as if he didn't care. I guess I should be disappointed with me too. I'd considered calling this off more than once today but then would that be me making the decision or Eli making it. I wasn't sure so I stuck with it. What could it hurt really? My pride was obviously already gone.

The blue sleeveless sundress I was currently wearing hit just at my knees. I liked it. This was comfortable and could go either dressy or casual. I wouldn't be changing my clothes again. That was something a girl excited about a date did. I wasn't excited.

One last time I walked into the living room and stood between Eli and the television. Nate would be here any minute.

"You can ignore me all you want but that's silly. I know this is a bad idea. It's stupid. But I need to do it. So, stop trying to protect me and let me do things. Make mistakes. The whole shebang. Okay?"

For a moment, I thought he was going to continue to ignore me but he let out a frustrated sound that was something like a sigh. "Fine."

That was all I needed. "Thank you."

He didn't look amused. He just shook his head. "The guy is a dick."

It was right there on the tip of my tongue. I wanted to defend him. To tell Eli that Nate wasn't a bad guy. But I didn't. It wasn't my place to defend him. Eli could think what he wanted. Nate would be gone soon anyway.

The knock at the door stopped us from having anymore conversation and Eli took a drink of his water. He was done talking about it anyway. "See you later. I doubt I'm gone long."

He just nodded.

I didn't have time for this. I grabbed my purse and went to open the door.

As it swung wide I almost wished I hadn't opened it at all. I wished I had called and canceled. It would have saved me a lot of issues. Like the major issue being Nate Finlay was beautiful. Model perfect. He was rugged yet refined. Beautiful but handsome. He was mouthwatering. And I had to remember he was only taking me out because I forced him to.

"Hey," he said with a grin that made my heart go all silly and fluttery. Dang it. My entire body was going to betray me.

"Hi. You're on time," I replied. That was stupid. I was nervous. Why was I nervous? This was Nate. This date meant nothing. I shouldn't be doing this. He was here because I all but drug him here. I hated that feeling. He was so perfect and I was . . . well me.

I didn't want this memory of him. I had too many memories that I cherished. This could ruin it all. What had I been thinking?

"I changed my mind. I think this is a bad idea. Thanks for doing it though but I don't want to go out with a guy I forced to take me."

Eli's eyes were on me. They were burning a hole in my back. I could feel him. I bet he spun around the moment the first couple of words tumbled out of my mouth.

"I don't do things I don't want to do. And after seeing you in that dress, with your pretty hair in curls, there is no way I am walking away. You wanted this and now, so do I."

I hadn't expected that response. My mind had been prepared to see him walk away with a "so long". This surprised me. He wanted to go out.

"Really?" was the brilliant word that came out of my mouth then. Not "thank you" or something more . . . I don't know intelligent maybe. I just said "really?"

He chuckled. "Yeah, most definitely."

Okay. Well then that changed everything. He was here looking like sex on a stick and he wanted me to go out with him. Our one last memory to satisfy me for the rest of my life. I was still pathetic but I was going. I was over feeling sorry for myself. Besides, he thought my curls were pretty.

"Well, okay, um, well, yeah, I guess I'm ready then," I was rambling like a lunatic. God help me this was just getting worse.

He tilted his head toward the parking lot with a sexy jerk. Very Nate Finlay. He always made the simplest things appear cool. "Come on."

I stepped outside and I didn't look back at Eli. I wasn't ready for that look of his. The one where he wasn't falling for Nate's charm. He wasn't a female. He didn't understand.

"I'm glad you wanted this," Nate said as the door closed.

"You are?"

"Yeah. I am."

That was enough talk. It eased my tension and once again I was with Nate. The guy I knew. The guy I had loved. The guy whose memory got me through the darkest days of my life. This was right. It always felt right with him.

"Are you and Octavia actually broken up?" I asked needing to know I wasn't doing something wrong.

"Oh, yeah. That's done."

I was grinning. The guy had just broken up with his fiancé the night before and I wasn't able to hide my pleasure. God help me, I needed classes on how to date. I sucked at it.

~NATE FINLAY~

IF THIS NIGHT could be frozen in time. Nothing before, nothing after. Just this one night be all there was, I could die happy.

Because it was as close to perfect as I would ever get. Problem was the reality would come. And with it a truth neither of us was ready for.

I'd wanted Bliss alone. None of her friends showing up and taking my limited time with her away. Yes, it sounded controlling and jealous but all I had was tonight and I wasn't willing to share. I knew before it even started that this was it. All I would get.

During our private dinner on the rooftop of hotel owned by my Uncle Grant, I did everything I could to make her laugh. Bliss's laughter was infectious. Hearing her made me smile. The need to laugh and feel free of any darkness threatening to step in and end this was strong but not strong enough. Because I knew the truth I knew the reality. I was just glad she didn't. At least for now. Tomorrow or the day after she'd know. And with that I'd never see her again.

She was drying the tears brought on by laughter from her eyes and I just watched in awe. I'd never known a girl like Bliss. Everything you saw was exactly what she was. There was nothing there she was hiding or insecure about. She was just herself and she was comfortable in her own skin. What would my life be like if I could spend every day with her? Would it be different? Would I be different?

"Tell me about your first date then. You've had enough fun laughing at mine," she said leaning forward with her smile illuminated in the moonlight. The kind of moment that could last you a lifetime.

"No way. Yours was funny but mine was just embarrassing," I said standing up then holding my hand out to take hers. She slipped her hand into mine so trusting and stood up.

"That's not fair! Mine was embarrassing!"

Hers was cute and innocent. Mine ended with me ejaculating before I could get my dick into Haley Martin's older experienced vagina. That had been embarrassing. But when you're a sixteen-year-old boy and an eighteen-year-old with big tits and porn quality features gets naked in your car and asks you to fuck her it's a little too exciting to keep from exploding early. Bliss however wouldn't get the humor in all that. And I wasn't about to tell her.

"I'd rather look at the stars with you," I replied and pulled her over to the lounger sofa that I had made sure faced the water and the moonlight. This was what Bliss needed. Romance. She wasn't like the other females I'd had in my life. I couldn't bend her over that sofa and bury myself inside her while we looked at those stars. Although to me that sounded pretty damn romantic. Bliss deserved more. She needed the romance to go with the sex.

We sat down and I put my arm around her shoulders pulling her against my side. There were a million things I could have asked her. Several topics available to me so why the fuck I asked "When was the first time you had sex?" I do not know. But I did.

She jerked her head around to look at me wide eyed then she laughed. Thank God she thought this was funny and not getting all stiff and uncomfortable with me. That would suck. I wanted her warm and relaxed in my arms. She smelled wonderful and this would just be another of those things I stocked back for days when I needed to feel happy. This memory would give me that.

"Are you planning on asking me questions all night and not answering any yourself? I should at least get your first sex story. If I'm not going to get your first date story."

"One and the same," I replied.

Her big eyes went even wider and then she covered her mouth as she laughed. "You had sex on your first date?"

I shrugged. It had been something I liked to brag about in the field house at school but with Bliss I wasn't about to recap.

"You have to tell me now. That's just not fair."

She was wanting my first sex story. Bliss was an adult now. She wasn't that sweet innocent girl I'd fallen in love with. Any other girl had asked me to tell her this I would have and given them details. Was it right for me to treat Bliss like she was innocent and breakable? She didn't want that obviously.

"You really want to hear this?"

She nodded her head turning her body toward mine and pressing her chest against my arm. That was a little distracting but I didn't let my eyes go to her low cut dress and enjoy the view. Talking about sex with Bliss was going to make me fucking hard.

"She was eighteen. I was sixteen," I began.

I expected Bliss to jump in here with a comment on the age difference but she stayed silent. So, I went on.

"We went to the movies and I can't remember what we saw because she kept slipping her hand up my thigh then took my hand and slipped it under her skirt. I was sixteen and all I could think about was the fact I could possibly be losing my virginity that night."

Bliss laughed softy, so I went on.

"We didn't make it to the end of the movie. Once I got my hand under her skirt she spread her legs and well, it didn't take long for her to be ready to leave."

"Did you touch her . . . like without the panties there as a barrier?"

Jesus. That one question from her and my dick was so damn hard I could break shit with it.

"Uh, she wasn't wearing panties. One of the reasons Haley's skirts were famous at school was when she bent over or opened her legs you had a clear view. The male teachers and a couple of the female teachers enjoyed it as much as we did."

"Oh my god," Bliss said but she didn't sound horrified. She was fascinated. The little freak. Grinning I rested my hand on her thigh to keep from losing my mind if I didn't touch something other than her shoulders.

"I actually heard Coach J say the same thing once in his office about five minutes before Haley walked out wiping the corners of her mouth and smiling."

Bliss grabbed my arm. "She gave the coach a blow job?"

I nodded. "Several I'm sure. Coach J was younger and the girls loved him."

"So what happened when you left the movie?"

Bliss was too into this. I was supposed to be romantic and give us both a memory to keep. Not tell her sex stories. But damn if her interest wasn't turning me on. I was enjoying this as much if not more than her.

"We, uh, you sure you want to hear this?"

She nodded again so I continued.

"We made it to my car, it was a Range Rover back then. She crawled in the backseat and got naked. I followed her and got my clothes off as fast as I could. She slid a condom down over my dick which was good because I wasn't sure how to do it. Then she climbed on top of me straddling my waist and well, her boobs were in my face and her pussy started down on my dick and I fucking blew right there. Luckily I had on the condom. It wasn't my finest hour."

Bliss giggled and I had to smile. I had never admitted that to anyone before. With Bliss, everything just seemed right.

Chapter Sixteen

❤ BLISS YORK ❤

I DIDN'T HAVE a promise of another night with Nate. It was me who had made this date happen. By force. Just because we were having a good time or at least I thought he was, didn't mean I'd get another date. He said he was leaving Sea Breeze.

Listening to him talk about sex had made my body tingle in areas that wanted a release of their own. But how did I tell him that? I wasn't one to take off all my clothes and climb in his truck. Although I wish I were. I wanted to experience sex with Nate. I'd never had sex but I wanted to. With Nate.

His hand was on my thigh so I did the only thing I could think of. I put my hand on his and slid his hand up my thigh and then pressed it between my thighs. He had gone still beside me. I wasn't sure he was even breathing. My heart was beating so rapidly in my chest from nerves and excitement I could hear it.

"Bliss," he said my name in a deeper tone as his hand flex and griped my inner thigh.

"Yes," I replied in a whisper.

"Are you sure?" he asked.

"Yes," I said again.

He didn't need more than that. His body turned and covered mine as we lay there on the lounger. This time when his lips touched mine I knew it wasn't for a moment. There was no guilt. I sank my fingers into his hair and held on while his hard, warm body moved over me. This was what it was supposed to be like. This was why I never let it get far with other guys. I wanted Nate. I imagined this was Nate. I had since I was fifteen years old.

One of his hands cupped my face while the other ran down my body feeling and brushing the right places. I wish I had gotten naked first. The touch of his hand on my skin would be amazing. I squirmed at the thought and the hardness of his erection touched my leg. I froze then. I wanted to rub against it. Feel more of it but this was all new to me and I wasn't sure.

Nate's tongue slipped inside my mouth and his taste excited me further. When he pressed his erection against me, I made a sound I didn't recognize. But he'd pressed it right where I needed to feel it. Right where my body was aching for contact.

If I was naked right now this would be perfect.

"Bliss," he said my name against my skin as his mouth moved from mine to trailed kisses down my neck. I arched against him and his hand slid under my dress and moved further up my body caressing my stomach before covering my breast. Nate had touched me here before. But then I'd been young and we had experimented mostly. Not really known what to do. I still didn't.

My legs fell open so that he could fit inside them closer. And I could feel more. Instead he moved back away from me and I started to protest just before he took the hem of my dress and jerked it up my body. I lifted my arms so he could take it off me without needing to be told.

His shirt followed then he began unfastening his pants. Maybe I wasn't supposed to look but I was fascinated with watching him. I'd never seen a man naked. This would be my first. Just like everything he did Nate had his jeans off with a smooth ease that wasn't awkward at all. It should have been but it wasn't.

Then he was back over me. His boxer briefs still in place. My panties and bra still there as barriers. I didn't want a barrier. I wanted to feel it all. But the thrill of the skin on skin contact I did get had me forgetting everything else.

Nate kissed my stomach and the curves of my breasts before reaching around and unhooking the offending object to discard it. Now I felt naked. Bared. He stared at me a moment and during that time I wanted to cover myself. What if I wasn't enough? What if I didn't meet his expectations?

"This . . . is better than I imagined. And I imagined it a lot. A whole fucking lot."

I smiled then. It was as if he knew what I needed to hear. The sweet reassurance made me love him more.

"I don't have a condom," he said as he reached for my panties and began to move them down my legs. "So I'll be leaving my boxers on."

I could tell him that I'd never get pregnant. I couldn't. I had survived cancer but it had taken so much from me. The one thing that hurt the most was that I'd never be able to carry a child inside me. Reminding him of my sickness at this moment. I didn't want to do that.

My thoughts had started to go dark with that reminder when he moved my legs over his shoulders. This I knew . . . I'd read about it in books. I was aware of what he was doing but I was suddenly terrified.

He didn't give me long to think it through before his tongue touched my center and my hips bucked off the lounger and a cry of pleasure came from my mouth. All the reasons this scared me were gone. I grabbed the back of his head with my hands and held him there. Not caring if that was wrong or if I was doing something I shouldn't. I would do whatever he wanted if he'd just keep kissing me there. Tasting me. I knew what an orgasm was. I'd given myself plenty. So I recognized what my body was climbing toward. However, it had never felt like this. My fingers never brought my body to this trembling ball of explosives that were threatening to ignite at any time. I wanted it and then I also wanted this to go on forever. I was torn between what it would bring me and wanting to keep feeling this.

He ran a hand up my inner thigh and pushed my legs open further exposing me completely to him. Watching his head buried there was all I could take. The release that came was like nothing I'd ever known. I cried his name over and over as my body went from trembling to shaking.

His mouth thankfully released me or I was sure I'd die from the sensitive pressure it left behind. He kissed his way back up my body and then he tucked his face in my neck.

"Jesus, you taste good."

"And you . . . uh," I had to pause to catch my breath. "You're really good at that."

He chuckled again my skin. "Thanks."

I could still feel his erection against my hip.

"I can . . . um . . . do the same." How did one ask to give a guy a blow job? And was I even going to know what I was doing? Did I lick it? Or did you really suck it like a lollypop? I wished I knew more. Wasn't so damn clueless.

"Bliss," he said lifting his head to look at me. "Are you offering to suck my dick?"

That was one way to put it. I nodded.

He didn't move for a moment. I was torn between hoping he said no thanks because I wasn't sure how this worked to being worried he didn't want me to because I had done something to turn him off.

"If I was a gentleman I'd say no that's okay. You don't have to but fuck that," he said moving back and pulling off his boxers. His erection stood straight and it was huge. I mean I had never actually seen a penis but I didn't realize they were so large. How was I supposed to get that all in my mouth?

"There is nothing more I'd rather see in this life than your head over my lap with your mouth full of my cock."

The area between my legs came back to life after already having its turn at fun. Why was Nate talking dirty exciting me?

~NATE FINLAY~

I STILL HAD the taste of her orgasm in my mouth as Bliss lowered her head over my dick. If I'd had a fucking condom I would have her sweet ass bent over and I'd be buried inside that wet pussy right now. But I didn't.

Her tongue slid over the head and I shook. I sure as hell couldn't take her teasing me. It was taking all my willpower not to grab her head and shove that sexy little mouth down over my cock. I didn't want to choke her . . . well, now that was a lie. The idea of chocking her with my dick was exciting. Hearing her gag with it in her throat was hot as hell. But she seemed nervous. I didn't want to scare her. Because she might stop and Jesus, I didn't want her to stop.

Her tongue trailed down each side and my hands were literally trembling. I balled them into fists. I'd had my dick sucked a lot and by some pros but none of them compared to it being Bliss. Even if she hadn't actually sucked it yet. Her prep work was about to kill me.

After she had thoroughly licked it and I was on the verge of begging her to stick it in her mouth she tilted her head back and looked up at me. "I've . . . do I . . . is this right? Or do I actually suck on it?" her cheeks were flushed and her words slowly sank in. She'd never done this before.

The image of Bliss's mouth being on some other guy's dick wasn't appealing and now knowing it never had been thrilled me. It shouldn't. She wasn't mine but damn I liked this.

I touched her head gently. "Slowly put it in your mouth. Get as much in it as you can take then suck it."

Explaining this to her was a fucking turn on. As if I needed anything more to make me want her. She put both her hands on it and then finally my dick sank into her mouth. The wet warmth and the way her tongue flicked it as it moved deeper felt incredible.

"Yeah, that's it." Fuck! That was it. I touched her head but I didn't let myself shove down on it like I wanted to.

She continued to do as I told her and with each groan and word of praise out of my mouth she got more sure of herself. Soon she was taking me deeper in her throat and I knew I couldn't shoot my load in her mouth. Not if this was her first time. But damn the image of it made my cock throb.

"Fuck, Bliss, yeah baby," I was lost in a level of heaven I didn't want to leave. Ever. What would happen tomorrow and the future didn't seem to matter anymore. Not when Bliss was sucking on the head and jacking me off with her hand.

Squeezing my eyes shut I tried to hold off. I didn't want to end this but the end was there and I grab my dick and move her head back. "I'm coming," I managed to get out just as my load erupted all over her bare chest. She watched me coat her tits with such wide-eyed innocence I came just little harder at the sight of it.

"Fuuuck," I groaned and my release began to roll down over a nipple. I'd never forget the way she looked right now.

She lifted her eyes to meet mine then she smiled. It was the happy pleased kind that made me laugh.

"Wow," she said and I laughed some more.

"I didn't mean to coat you with it," I told her.

She beamed at me. "I like that you did. It felt good."

I was getting hard again. Jesus, she needed to shut up. We couldn't have sex.

"Stay right there," I said standing up and going over to the table to get one of the linen napkins and a glass of water. She needed to be cleaned up.

When I knelt in front of her to clean her up she arched her back to let me. And my thickening dick got even harder. "I might need to let you do this," I told her. "Because this . . . you doing that . . . I want to fuck you. ."

Her cheeks were flushed. I wasn't sure if it was all the sucking or my words causing it but I liked it.

"Then do."

No, no, no, no. I shook my head and handed her the napkin before moving away. "Not happening."

I didn't watch her clean herself. I couldn't. Or we would be fucking.

"You don't have to come inside me."

She wanted me to pull out. Motherfucker I wanted to. I knew I was clean and after that blow job experience I knew her experience was limited so she was clean. But damn . . . what if? That was a chance I wasn't sure we should take.

"Not a good idea," I told her and reached for my boxers to get myself covered back up before the temptation was too great.

"Okay," she finally said and I turned to look back at her. She was still naked and she hadn't got all my come off her chest yet.

"Bliss," my tone was warning.

"Yes."

"Cover up. Get dressed. You don't want to play this game with me."

She didn't move. "Yes I do."

Fuck. Fuck. Fuck.

I started to just leave. Walk away and send a car to get her. That was what I should do. But as I moved I was moving toward her. I jerked her up and pulled her against my chest before kissing her with all the desire and frustration she had built up in me. It was hard and too rough but she kissed back just as fiercely and I couldn't make the right decision. I couldn't walk away.

I broke the kiss and shoved her back on the lounger. Taking both her legs I held them open and looked at her there like that. Her eyes wide with excitement. I was doing this. When I knew, I shouldn't. I was doing it.

The boxers I had just put on I was out of immediately and with one thrust of my hips I was buried inside her. The cry of pain and thin barrier told me something I should have figured out. I should have known. But damn she was a woman now. I didn't expect that.

A blow job being her first was one thing but sex? The caveman took over. I wanted to beat on my chest and say "mine" but that wasn't possible. I had to leave. She couldn't be mine. She deserved her prince.

I ran my hand over her head and looked down at her. Tears pooled in her eyes and I knew it was from the pain. If I'd known I could have been easier. But then if I'd known would I have done this?

"Take a deep breath. I won't move until it eases."

She inhaled deeply and kept her eyes on me. "It's just a little sting now."

I moved so that the pleasure would increase and take the pain away sooner.

Her breathing became panting and I moved faster. The tightness of her virgin entrance squeezing me so hard that I wanted to blow again too soon. When she began to tremble in my arms and her eyes closed I knew her orgasm was there. I bit my tongue to keep from going off with her.

"AH! Ohgod!" she cried and I held her as she broke apart in my arms. When she was still lost in her euphoria I had to jerk my hips out before it was too late. Holding my dick, I yelled out my release as my come shot all over her thighs.

The traces of blood were there on my skin and the inside of her thighs. Mixed with my semen. Making her mine when I knew she never would be.

Chapter Seventeen

♥ BLISS YORK ♥

I DIDN'T LOOK different. Did I? Standing in my bathroom I studied myself. Would Eli know? Surely not. I didn't want to talk to him about this. I touched my bare stomach and smiled. Nate Finlay had kissed me there. I had been kissed all over by him. When he'd brought me back last night he had kissed me so gently as if I might break.

Then he had said he'd call me today. What had started as a mistake or what I thought was a mistake had ended wonderfully. I had got my date with Nate and somehow I'd got Nate too. After all these years, we were together again. My heart felt full as if it could burst with all the joy pumping through it right now. I was happy. Truly happier than I'd ever been. Last night had been everything I hoped for. Had dreamed about. Yes, it hurt but the pain had eased and it felt amazing.

Even the tenderness down there this morning was nice. It reminded me of Nate and what we had shared. I didn't really have anyone I could tell about this. But I didn't want to. I wanted it to be our private moment. Telling a friend all about it would take away from how special it had been.

Maybe I did look different. I sure felt different. More complete. As if my body knew it had just changed dramatically. That it would never be the same.

"Got coffee made. You want eggs?" Eli called through the door.

No. Yes. I was hungry but facing Eli wasn't something I was ready for. He would ask about last night and I'd have a goofy smile on my face. He'd know something. What if he guessed? I looked at my reflection in horror. That was not going to happen. I'd be ready to talk to him in a day or two.

But not now.

"Thanks but I'm going to see mom," I called back. Which I hadn't been planning on that but now it seemed like it was the only thing I wanted to do. I couldn't tell her but just seeing her and maybe asking some sex questions and relationship questions might help. She was the only one I had to ask. That I trusted what she had to say.

"Oh. Okay. Do you work tonight?"

I did. I didn't want to. I wanted to see Nate. But I had a job and I had to be there. "Yeah. Seven to close."

"I'll see you tonight then. I've got to work all day."

Eli had a job working at his grandfather's car lot. He did computer filing and handled their social media. It was an easy gig but I wasn't jealous. He had offered me a job there too. I just wouldn't take it. I knew they didn't need me. I didn't want them making a job up for me.

"Okay. I'm getting in the shower. If you're gone when I get out I'll see you tonight."

I turned on the water needing to end this conversation. It was awkward because I knew he was wanting to ask me about last night but wouldn't. He wanted me to just tell him.

This time Eli didn't get to know everything.

Pulling into my parents' driveway always made me feel safe. I hadn't been moved out long but I knew this would always be my home. The boys' community truck was gone so they had already left for school. I had timed it just right. Dad would be working and the boys were gone.

I liked to see my brothers and father but I wanted mom to myself. I wasn't even to the door when it opened and she stepped out onto the wide wrap around porch. The smile on her face was big and beautiful just like her. I had always thought I had the prettiest mother.

"I have company I wasn't expecting. Good thing I made extra biscuits." Momma always made extra biscuits. She grew up on this farm feeding her grandfather and the workers. It was what she did. Having a husband and three boys to feed made her happy.

"What about tomato gravy? Got any of that?" I asked.

She nodded. "Of course I do."

"Then I'm starving."

She wrapped her arms around me when I stepped up onto the porch. "I miss seeing this face every day. Takes all my willpower not to ride into Sea Breeze just to see you. But you look good. You look happy.

"I am happy," I assured her. Now if she'd asked me this time yesterday I wouldn't have been able to say the same thing. At least not honestly.

"Come inside and let me feed you while you tell me what or who has that smile on your face," she said opening the door for us to go inside.

"I had a date last night," I decided against telling her that I forced that date.

"Oh, with who?"

"Nate Finlay," I replied.

She paused. "What about his fiancé?"

"They broke it off. After I quit my job. It all kind of snow-balled."

We stepped inside and mom wasn't saying much. I knew she was thinking this through. Like Eli she didn't want me hurt. But unlike Eli she was more careful how she handled it. I waited for her to decide what she was going to say next.

Walking over to get a cup out of the cabinet for my coffee, I was holding my breath. I wanted her to be happy for me. But I wasn't sure she would be. This wasn't an ideal situation. But it was what I wanted.

"Did he break it off, or did she?" mom finally asked.

"He did."

"For you"

"No." I replied watching her face for any hint of what she was thinking.

"Then why?"

"Because he wanted more. They were weird together. No connection. No attachment. She didn't even seemed to care when he broke things off. It was similar to the way she acted when I quit."

Mom didn't fix my plate. She sat down letting me help myself. Which was normal in this house. Momma raised us to take care of ourselves. "Are you happy with him"

That was an easy question. "Very."

She sighed and put both her hands around the cup of coffee in front of her. "That's good. I want you happy. I want you to have it all. But I don't want you hurt and prepare yourself this could hurt you. It seems odd for her to take the breakup that easily."

"You don't know what she's like. She's self-centered and it was never a real relationship anyway."

Mom just nodded. "Okay."

She didn't go into it any deeper but I could see the look in her eyes. She wasn't convinced. "Well, tell me all about the date.

I want to know if he was everything you hoped he would be."

He had been more. But I wasn't telling her everything. There were some things a mother didn't need to know. I did want to talk about him though. I wanted to smile and feel giddy. I wanted to tell her all about how it happened and how what I thought was a mistake ended up being perfect.

~NATE FINLAY~

I SHOULD LEAVE. Bliss deserved more than what I wanted. But fuck me if I could make myself walk away from her. I'd stayed up most of last night replaying every moment in my head. It had been the best date of my life and although Bliss was the marriage, babies, and picket fence kind of girl I was still unable to leave her alone.

Hell, maybe I could do that shit. Settle down and not travel the world. Live in a small town and raise kids. If I got to have sex like that every day and hear her sweet laugh then it was worth it. The life I had planned for myself wasn't exactly happy. It was lonely. Full of adventure but lonely.

She had me talking crazy. I stared out the window of my Grandpop's condo and watched the waves crash on the shore. I wondered if she was here. Just a floor up in her room. If I left right now and didn't come back how would she feel? Would she hate me? Probably. She should hate me. I'd hate me.

No. I couldn't leave. I had to stay. See if this would be more. If this was what I was searching for when I thought, it was adventure I wanted. This could be an adventure. Bliss may travel. She may want to see things and explore places. I was assuming she wanted the slow life in a small town. I didn't know that.

I picked up my phone. I said I'd call today. This was my

moment. Did I call and stay? Or did I run and not look back? Then regret it for the rest of my life.

I pressed her saved number and waited. On the third ring:

"Hello"

"Good morning. Did you sleep good." I could see myself in the mirror's reflection. I was smiling. Her voice made me smile. Why would I run from that?

"Yes and you?"

Not a fucking wink. "Yeah, slept great. Have you had breakfast?" it was almost lunch time. Unless she was lazy then she'd had breakfast.

"Just left my parents' house. Mom had leftovers from breakfast and we visited."

She had that life. The same kind I had. We talked about it often when we were younger. How normal our lives were and how we had good parents. I was glad she had that. If she'd had sucky parents would she have survived?

"I'm available for lunch though. I work tonight."

She would be at Live Bay. I wouldn't have her all to myself. That put me in a bad mood. I was getting in deep if that bothered me. The girl had to work. I didn't need to get all moody about it.

"If you're working tonight then can I have you all day?"

There was a soft laugh on the other line. "Yes." Her tone was pleased and I hoped that meant she liked the idea of me having her. Because now all I could think about was bending her over the sofa and fucking her sexy sweet ass.

"I'll be back home in about twenty minutes. When do you want to meet?"

I wasn't going to be able to eat with the need to touch her this strong. "Come to my grandpop's condo. We'll make plans then."

There was a pause and a hitch in her breath. She was a smart girl. She knew what I wanted and she wanted it to. Thank god.

"Okay."

We ended the call and I continued to stare. I had my mind on other things now. Like her body and how perfectly it fit mine. No man in his right mind could walk away from that. He wouldn't want to.

This life . . . suddenly felt really fucking appealing. Or was it the need for Bliss's body that was changing my mind? I hadn't wanted Octavia this way. Sure she was a freak. I'd done some crazy porn worthy things with her. But it was different. There was a missing piece and I now knew it was that connection. The one I had with Bliss. The one I'd always had with Bliss.

Octavia's need to fuck in public places where she knew some-one might see us had grown annoying. She got off on being watched. I liked that shit at first but then she started pushing it too far. Like wanting to do it at the shop hoping Bliss would see us. I wasn't about to go there. The last thing I had wanted Bliss to see was me fucking Octavia.

The first time she wanted to do it, we did it in the men's restroom at a club. With a guy who walked in watching. She told me to go harder when the guy came in and she became a maniac while he watched. He'd started jacking off while watching us and that made her come. None of us were anywhere near sober but that night I was sure I could live with Octavia the rest of my life.

I'd been wrong. Kinky sex hadn't been enough. I was reminded of that the moment those boxes fell and Bliss was standing there looking wide eyed and shocked. Deeper meaning had come back to me and I had been fighting it ever since.

The knock on my door brought me back to the here and now. I went to open it and Bliss standing there in a short soft pink sundress with no bra on underneath was all I needed.

"Are you wearing panties?" I asked taking her hand and pulling her in the condo then slamming the door behind her.

"Of course."

I reached under her short dress and tore the small flimsy satin panties off. "Good," was my response. "Are you sore?"

She blushed. "A little."

I pushed her back against the door and dropped to my knees. Taking one of her legs I threw it over my shoulder and gently began kissing the pink sensitive flesh I'd had the night before.

"Nate," she breathed and her head hit the door with a thump. "I don't know if I can stand while you do this."

I began working her clit with my tongue and she panted my name along with god's name. It was adorable and made me want to tease her more. I was actually down here to make it all feel better so I could bury myself inside again. Now. Soon.

I didn't need someone to watch us to get me off. Or get her off. I was throbbing with excitement just from the smell of her.

Her legs wobbled and she leaned forward and her hands grabbed my shoulders. I gave her one last lick before dropping her leg and standing up.

"I want to fuck you, Bliss. Not the sweet loving we did last night. I want to bend you over and grab your hips and fuck your pussy from behind."

If I was going to scare her that kind of talk should do it. Instead she was still panting. "Okay. Do you want me to bend over here?"

This time, not laughing at that innocent question was hard. But I didn't. She was being sincere and I didn't want to laugh at her.

I grabbed her hand and pulled her over to the sofa. She wasn't going to be able to stand for this. Not if my eating her pussy had her almost ready to collapse in the floor. "Get on your knees and lean over the back of the sofa."

She did as I told her and I jerked her dress up exposing her ass to me. I was going to come on that ass. Watch it run down her crack. Jerking my sweats down I was already naked underneath. I stepped out of them and moved in behind her.

"Pull your arms out of your straps and let your tits free. I want to be able to grab them."

Chapter Eighteen

♥ BLISS YORK ♥

HIS LARGE HANDS grabbed my waist with more strength than I expected. It was startling yet exciting. My heart was racing and I wasn't sure what to expect. There had been a tender throb between my legs all day and the idea of him going back in had made me nervous. But after he had worked his magic down there with his mouth it was all I could think about.

The pain was more pleasure than anything. My body was craving the same release it got last night and I held onto the sofa anxious to be filled with him.

"Spread your legs more and stick up your ass," his words were thick and deep. I was ready to beg him so I did exactly as I was told. Whatever got him inside me I would do.

The moment my bottom was pushed up his hands squeezed my hips and he was inside. One hard move like last night and I was full. This time there was no searing pain. A little sting but no more. There was a constant ache down there wanting him to do more. Give me more.

"Fuck that's a tight pussy," he growled. "Needs to be fucked. It's my tight pussy. It'll know my fucking dick. You'll get wet thinking about how good this feels. How much you want it."

He was right on all accounts. I was having trouble breathing. I couldn't say anything back. His hands came around and grabbed my breasts and squeezed them. That sent an electric tingle through my body and right down to my clit. How had I missed this for so many years? No wonder girls in high school got pregnant. If this was what sex was then I understood their weakness. I may follow Nate around begging for it like a puppy dog.

He pinched my nipples and I cried out as he began moving harder inside me. Each time he entered there was more force behind it and that brought me closer to my orgasm. His grunts and the feel of his hand roughly touching me. Like he can't get enough of me was intoxicating.

"When I come I'm shooting it all over your ass. Round little ass will be covered with my load. Fucking perfect." If it wasn't his body taking me closer to heaven it was his dirty words. The way he sounded as wild for me as I was for him.

"Oh god," I cried as the first tremor ran through my body. I would promise him anything at this moment. I would give him anything at this moment if he just didn't stop. If this crash that was coming washed all over me and sent me back to that euphoria. "Please," I begged as the pull came for me. "Harder!" I cried out.

"You want it harder? Hot little pussy wants it harder I'll fucking give it to you harder. He began pumping so hard I felt his balls slap my clit and that was it. I broke into a million pieces and screamed out as the orgasm claimed me.

"That's it," Nate encouraged then he pulled out and yelled.

"FUUUUUCK!" I felt the warmth of his come as it covered my bottom. Laying my head down on the back of the sofa I tried to catch my breath. My ass was stuck up in the air covered in come. I was sweating. And I didn't care. My body was recovering and it felt wonderful.

"Not sure I'll ever be able to go in public with you," he said after a few moments of silence.

"Why?"

"Because I want to keep you naked and my dick buried inside you."

Smiling, I bit my bottom lip. That didn't sound like a bad idea to me.

His fingers brushed my extremely sensitive opening and I jumped.

He chuckled. "Just making sure I didn't hurt it."

"Oh you did. And you can hurt it again when you're ready."

"You're going to kill me," he said teasingly as he wiped my bottom clean. When he was done, I rolled over and sat down not bothering to pull my sundress up to cover myself. I still didn't have the energy.

He smiled at me and didn't bother to cover himself at all as he sank down beside me on the sofa. "Now I'm hungry."

I was too. All that had made me work up an appetite. "I could use some nourishment."

"We could order in or go out. You choose."

If we went out then I'd have to share him. I just got him. I wasn't ready to share him yet. Tonight I'd be working and we wouldn't have any alone time together.

"Order in."

He laughed letting his head fall back on the sofa. "I'm glad you want it as much as I do. Because once I recover I'm taking you to the shower."

I shivered from excitement. All wet and soapy sounded fun.

"Okay."

"But would you cover those tits so I can at least give my dick a break. It's already getting hard again."

Only because I needed a break myself. I slipped my arms back in my straps and covered myself. "Your grandfather isn't going to come home is he?"

"Nope. He only comes home on Sundays."

That was a relief. I didn't think his grandfather walking in on us fornicating would go over well.

"When will you be going home?" I asked it even though I didn't want to know. He couldn't live here . . . or he could but would he? Rosemary Beach wasn't that far but it wasn't like having him in the same building either.

"Not sure. When I do, maybe you could come too. And visit."

I hadn't been expecting that. I would have to deal with leaving work but if I had a few weeks to save I could maybe manage a few days.

"I'd like that."

He didn't reply right away and the silence wasn't uncomfortable. We didn't have to talk to fill the time. We sat there instead. He grabbed a blanket and threw it over his lap then reached over to pull me to him before he picked up his phone and called to order us a pizza.

This felt right. Like it had always been. My heart had never been this happy before. There were a lot of unknowns but for right now life was perfect.

"Next week," he said. "Let's go to Rosemary Beach next week."

I didn't need to take off work that soon. But I could pick up some extra shifts maybe before then. "Okay." If he wanted me to go with him I would make it work.

~NATE FINLAY~

I HAD TWENTY-FOUR hours of sex experiences with Bliss. And each one had been amazing. However, that shower fuck may have been the best. She left to go get ready for work and I knew I'd end up there tonight. She was like a magnet and I was unable to stay away from her. Especially after she soaped me up, worked my cock, then wrapped her legs around me while I pounded her with it. She had to be sore. Hell, my dick was sore. But she cried out for it and clung to my shoulders then clawed me like she wanted me to just crawl inside her and live there.

If this was why men got married and settled down, then I completely got it. They found the hottest pussy attached to someone as sweet and beautiful as Bliss and they were begging to be tied down.

When I shot my load all over her stomach while she watched me I considered proposing right then. I didn't of course but hell if I didn't want to. She had looked up at me with her hair soaking wet from the shower smiling like my semen all over her stomach was the best thing ever.

Her leaving for work had sucked. I liked having her here with me. But she had a job and she needed the money. I couldn't just keep her. I had finished up my last semester of college in the fall and not even tried to get a job because I knew I was going to be helping Octavia open her new store.

That wasn't happening now and I needed to decide on what I was going to do. Leaving didn't sound appealing anymore. But I couldn't get a permanent job here. I needed something for the now. This was all new and I wanted to be near Bliss. To find out where we were going. Give this a chance.

I reached for my phone. Grandpop would probably have an

idea of where I could work. Until I knew where I was going to go. Or hell, if I was going to put down roots here.

My father's father set me up a trust fund after I was born as he did my sisters. It was there to get me started in life. I wanted to build something. Create something. I just wasn't sure what yet. I had a business degree. I had ideas but I wasn't sure what I wanted that money to go towards.

"You still at my place" was my grandpop's greeting.

"Yeah. Listen, I'm thinking of staying here at least for the summer. I need to get a job though and a place of my own. You know anyone looking for some summer help?"

He chuckled. "Hell yeah, me. Hours ain't great. You'll work a lot of late nights. But I pay good."

I didn't really want to work for my grandpop but he continued to talk and the enthusiasm in his voice at the idea of me working there was going to make it impossible to turn him down.

"You sure you aren't making up a job for me?" I asked him.

"Nope. I'll be hiring several new people this month."

I was going to have to do this. "Okay. Thank you. I need to go home next week and get some things. But I'll be back then and ready to start."

"As for a place to stay just stay at my place."

I thought of Bliss sticking her ass up on the sofa and knew there was no way I was giving that up every Sunday when Grandpop was home. "I better get my own place. I'll rent something."

Grandpop let out a holler then he laughed. "Guess this is about that girl then."

"Yeah it is."

"Good. Smartest thing you've done in awhile."

Figured he'd be happy about it. So would my mother. She'd be thrilled when she met Bliss.

Just as I hung up with my grandpop my phone buzzed in

my hand and I looked down to see a text from Octavia. I hadn't expected that. Nor had I wanted it.

"We need to talk."

No we didn't. What was said and done was over. "Don't think so."

I waited a moment and she replied.

"Please. I'm sorry. I was indifferent and hard to deal with. Let's talk."

If I had loved her this would be different. But what we had was empty and we were wasting both our time. It was easy and I no longer wanted easy. Not at that price. Being with Bliss was a different kind of easy. The kind that made me feel something inside.

"We didn't work. You know that as well as I do. I don't want what we had."

It was hard but you could talk to Octavia that way. She was blunt and harsh. No need to sugar coat things with her.

I waited for a response. When I didn't get one I dropped the phone and went to get dressed. I'd call my mom and tell her about my visit next week and my summer plans. She wasn't the kind to call and bother you all the time. She let me call her and because she was so easy to deal with I tried to keep her updated. Besides if I let her get too worried my dad would kick my ass.

Tonight I'd go to Live Bay. Get to know Bliss's friends and fit into her world. I wanted her to want this as much as I did. Because there was no turning back now. One of them may even know a place I could rent.

My phone buzzed and I ignored it. Octavia was saying something more. I didn't want to be mean but that was over. She needed to get that. I wasn't the guy for her. I never was.

I could tell her about Bliss and that would make her stop. Her pride wouldn't let her keep trying if she knew I had moved on.

Stepping into the bedroom I smiled at the messy bed. It was also wet from our soaked bodies getting out of the shower. Tonight I'd take her there. Sweet and slow. Not that she didn't seem to enjoy the rough stuff but she needed to be treated special too. If I could keep my dirty mouth from shooting off was the only thing.

Taking the wet sheets off I made plans for our evening.

Chapter Nineteen

♥ BLISS YORK ♥

I DIDN'T HAVE to see him walk in to know he was there. Although I'd been looking for him all night. It was well after ten. The place had been busy tonight. Larissa had me working the side of the room that had our bunch sitting in it. No one else wanted to deal with them when they were being rowdy like this.

Micah was arguing with Jude while Damon was flirting with Saffron. He knew better. But he was drunk. Holland had thankfully come tonight with Saffron. She was the only one quietly observing the wild mess going on at that table.

I had a tray full of drinks to deliver to them when I turned to see Nate headed my way. The smile was immediate. I couldn't help it. Seeing him made me all giddy and happy inside. It was like there was that summer and there was now. All that happened in-between was gone. No longer mattered.

"Hey," I said feeling shy allof the sudden.

He walked up to me slipped his hand around my back and kissed me. Right there. It wasn't a hot sexy kiss but a casual "hello this is my woman" kiss and I liked it.

"Hey," he said when he pulled back slightly then grinned.

"Sorry I'm late. Had to go to Grandpop's and workout some details of my new job with him."

His new job? "What?"

His smirk remained in place like he was enjoying the confusion on my face. "I needed a job and he offered me one. Said he needs extra help for the summer. Next step is finding a place to live. Know any good rentals?"

He was getting a job and a place to live. Holy crap! The smile that broke out on my face was all I could do. I had a tray full of drinks or I would have very likely thrown myself into his arms.

"You're staying?" That was very close to a squeal but I didn't care.

"Of course. I don't want to leave if this is where you are."

That said more than any other words he could have said.

"I really want to grab you and kiss your face," I told him.

"Let's get this tray to the table. You've stood there having to hold it long enough. Introduce me to your friends again because I don't think I've met all of them. The others, I don't remember names."

I had a definite pep in my step as we walked over to their table. Micah stood up and started taking everyone's drink order from my tray.

"Nate Finlay, did I just see you kissing our girl?" Micah asked sounding amused.

Before he had to respond I spoke up. "That one is Micah. You met him last time. This s Jimmy, you met him too but he was as drunk then as he is now so I doubt he remembers. Saffron, she hit on you. Her twin sister Holland who will not flirt so you don't have to worry about her. And Jude, Micah's brother. Eli who you know. Oh and Damon. Y'all this is Nate Finlay. My . . . friend." I wasn't sure what to call him but saying friend sounded weird.

"I'm your friend and you never sucked my face," Micah said

with a smirk.

"Shut up," Holland snapped at him. She was the quiet, nice twin but the girl also had a temper.

I didn't look at Eli because we hadn't talked about my date or anything so I didn't know how he'd feel about seeing the kiss before hearing how things were going. He could be odd about that kind of thing. Until Nate I had talked about most everything with Eli.

"Bliss!" Larissa was calling my name and I realized I'd taken too long.

"I gotta get back to work. Y'all don't tell Nate too much crap please," I said then turned to press a kiss to his cheek before running back to Larissa.

I was grinning like an idiot when I got to the bar.

"That boy rocked your world didn't he?" she asked when I got back to her.

"He's . . . I like him. Always have."

She laughed out loud. "I know that. I mean innocent Bliss isn't so innocent anymore. It's all over your face. I'm guessing a guy looks like that he knows what he is doing. Did you like it?"

She was talking about sex. I froze. I couldn't talk about this with her, could I? Was that disrespectful to Nate or would he care? I glanced back at him and saw Jimmy saying something that had everyone entertained.

"Yeah. I loved it." The words came out before I could stop them.

"Then he's a pro alright. First time sex isn't always good. It can be terrible. I had a friend who swore she'd never do it again after the first time. She did of course, eventually."

"I can't imagine not liking it."

Larissa laughed again. "Yeah, he's good. I'm happy for you Bliss. But right now, I need these drinks taken to table four. Then get the orders from six. They keep waving at me."

I hurried to do as she said trying hard not to look at Nate although I could feel his eyes on me. I liked knowing he was here watching me. What I liked even more was knowing I'd leave tonight and he'd go with me.

The next three hours went by in a blur. The place got packed and I didn't get to enjoy my stops to their table and get to visit with Nate.

It was an hour before closing time when I glanced back at Nate to see if he was still doing okay with my friends to see he was gone. I figured he'd gone to the restroom so I didn't think about it until he didn't come back.

My mind was racing with reasons why he left. I thought he would have come to tell me he was leaving. That didn't make sense for him to just leave. Unless someone said something to him.

I looked at Eli who was also looking at me and frowning. Had he said something to Nate? If he did, we were going to have an epic argument. He had no right to put his nose into my business. He also didn't know Nate. He just assumed he knew everything.

By the time my shift was over my mind had gone over a hundred different reasons why he left. I was mad at Eli by this point which was ridiculous. I had no idea if it was his fault. I needed to find out the reason first. Which meant I needed to go see Nate.

~NATE FINLAY~

THE BREEZE STILL blew, the water still crashed onto the shore, the sun still set and the moon still lit the evening sky. All of it was the same. It hadn't changed. Not once. It remained the very same. Just because a life was gone the world kept turning. That seemed unfair. But then it would be difficult to live on this earth if it mourned every life that was lost.

Still with one phone call my path had been jerked and turned. Where I had thought I was headed just hours ago, I knew now I never could. This would change me. Harden me. I'd never be able to forgive my choices. Or forget the two lives that were gone. One that I should have been given a choice over. One that was my right to choose.

Bliss was everything that was pure in this world. She was sunshine and happiness. She had walked through a hell of her own and came out still bright. Her outlook on life still optimistic. But that had been her battle and she'd won it.

I'd made one wrong move and my world would forever be altered. Bliss needed someone whole and I would never be. Not now. How could I? Why should I get to enjoy life when tragedy came to something that was mine to protect?

The duffel bag in my hand held my things. But it was like a led weight. Knowing when I drove away tonight I'd never be able to come back. Seeing Bliss and what I could have had would be too painful. The darkness that would now follow me wasn't fair to her.

"Nate?" her tone was nervous. She saw my bag. She knew without asking that I was leaving. What she didn't know was what I had done. How I had failed. The sorrow I'd forced to happen. My need for her, it had caused this. No one deserved this kind of lesson.

I couldn't force myself to turn around. I'd see her and the agony I was living through would get worse. Because I loved her. I would love her until the day I died. But she would always remind me of what I'd done. What my selfishness had caused.

"You're leaving," she said the words matter-of-factly but the emotion she held in check in her tone was something she couldn't mask.

"Yes." She deserved more than that. But saying the words. Admitting the horror . . . how did I do that?

"Did someone say something? If Eli said something he's an idiot. I'll deal with him. But whatever it is we can talk about it. There's no reason to leave."

She thought this was because of her. I guess in a way it was. My choice had been her. That had been what sparked the end result. But I couldn't blame her. She did nothing wrong. She was perfect and I was ruined. Broken. Fucking destroyed.

"Your friends said nothing. They were all welcoming. Friendly even."

God, how did I say this aloud?

"Then why? Did I do something wrong?" There was a crack in her voice. A small break. I was hurting her. I never wanted to hurt her. She should be held and loved. But a whole man was who she needed. I couldn't hold her and be happy.

"You did nothing. You are perfect." That wasn't her answer. I knew that. I had to tell her. To admit this. She should know the truth. Saying it was going to alter me even more. But I had no other choice. This would hurt her too but she'd know the truth and she'd move on with life. She'd find someone else to love. Someone who wasn't a shell of a man. Someone who could hold her without a darkness in their soul.

"My father called," I began. Fuck my throat was closing up. Breathing was hard. "They . . . her stepmother . . . Octavia's stepmother found her two hours ago. She . . ." God, I closed my eyes and inhaled deeply. The image was there in my head. Burned so deeply even though I hadn't seen it. The clarity of it and the pure horror wrecked me. "She was hanging from the banister of her father's home. A rope around her neck and a note." I had to stop there. My head pounded as those words repeated over and over in my head. The note. The pain in my father's voice as he told me.

"Oh mygod," Bliss whispered. Then her hand touched my arm and I jumped. Jerked away. Not now. She couldn't touch me now. She still didn't know it all. What would forever haunt me.

"Pregnant. She was four months pregnant," I swallowed the bile in my throat. With my baby. It was too small, underdeveloped to live outside of her body. They couldn't save it. She'd let the staff go home early. Said she was going to enjoy a quiet evening in. Her stepmother came home concerned when the housekeeper called her to tell her that Octavia had sent them all home." I wasn't breathing. I inhaled deeply again.

"Nate," she said softly and the sorrow in her voice was real. It wasn't the torture I would endure the rest of my life or the nightmare I would relive daily in my head. But I knew she understood.

"It was a boy," I had to say the last. Get it out. Acknowledge that I'd had a son. One that was taken from me. One I never got a chance to meet. One that didn't get a chance to come into this world His mother had made that choice for him. Saying this world was too cold a place and if she wanted to leave it then why would she bring a child into it.

There was silence. Nothing to say.

"You're gone then. For good," it wasn't a question. She was just confirming what she already knew.

"Yes."

I glanced at her briefly. Tears were streaming down her face as she mourned the lives lost. That was the last image I would ever have of her. Turning I walked away. From Sea Breeze. From happiness. From a life I would never deserve.

As I stepped into the parking lot I saw the familiar black G-Wagon that belonged to my father. He stepped out of the driver's side and my Uncle Grant stepped out of the passenger side. They both looked at me then my father started toward me.

When his arms wrapped around me I was five years old again and this was my safe place. But dad couldn't ease my heartache this time. "Grant's gonna drive your truck back. Get in the car with me," he said gruffly. He was hurting too. I'd caused all this. Me. And my fucking selfish need for a woman.

Chapter Twenty

❤ BLISS YORK ❤

I T WAS AS if my emotions were warring with each other over who would win. Who was the most powerful. I'm not sure how I walked back to my condo from the beach out front. I don't remember it. My thoughts were clouded with pain, sorrow, disbelief, and there was nothing I could do. Nothing I could say.

He hadn't wanted my comfort. There were no words I could have spoken that seemed right. No way to beg him not to leave me. To let me help him grieve. I couldn't grieve for him. This was a blow that went deep and brutal. I had faced death. And while facing it my concern had been for those I'd leave behind. The pain I would inflict. I had fought when I wasn't sure I had any fight left because I wouldn't let them suffer my death.

But Nate . . . he would have to live through not only the death of his child but a terrible tragedy. One that would wound him in a way I couldn't bear to think about. I wanted to be there for him. I hated letting him go. But he'd not wanted me.

Thinking about me and my loss wasn't fair. I wouldn't do that. I wouldn't hurt for me. Because I had loved a man and lost him. He had never even got to hold his son. I'd mourn but I'd mourn for him. Not because I lost him but because of what he lost. I loved Nate Finlay even if that love had been one sided. It was enough for me. I knew what love was. I had experienced it twice for very short times. But both with him.

The door opened and Eli was standing there. His face etched with worry and concern. "I saw him leave with two men. One drove him the other drove his truck. He had his duffel bag. Are you okay? What did he do?"

I just stood there trying to listen. Knowing I had to say something to Eli but my soul felt so fractured that it hurt to think. To stand. To speak.

"I swear to God I will track his sorry rich spoiled ass down and beat it! What did he do?"

Eli was angry. Worried that Nate had hurt me. He had but he had no other choice. He was hurting worse. I understood that.

"Octavia hung herself, Eli. And she was pregnant with his son."

Eli's anger blew out like a candle. His face dropped and the horror of my words registered on his face.

"Holy shit," he whispered.

"He's gone." Those two words didn't say everything but they didn't have to. Eli knew. Nate was gone and he wouldn't be back. I felt like a horrible person for even grieving over losing him. Before I even got to enjoy loving him.

Eli's arms were around me and once there I let the pain go. The sobbing for all Nate had lost. What he'd never have and for what we would never have.

I woke the next morning in my bed but my clothes were still on. Eli had held me while I cried last night on the sofa. That was the last thing I remembered. I must have fallen sleep. I touched my eyes. They felt raw and swollen. The ache in my chest was still there and I stared up at the ceiling. Today was like any other day. I'd get up, eat, get dressed, go to work. Life would go one. Except my heart was somewhere else. With someone else. And I couldn't help him. I couldn't hold him as Eli had held me

There was a soft knock on my door and then it slowly opened and Eli peeked in. "Oh you're awake," he said opening it wider and coming inside.

"I'll get you some coffee. What do you feel like eating?"

He was treating me like I had just lost my child. Like this horrific reality was mine. Who was making sure Nate had something to eat? Was there someone he would allow to hold him? Had he cried? Sobbed for the emptiness and grieved? Who was with him?

I hated this. I hated not knowing if he was okay. But he made it clear with his body language and words he didn't say that he didn't want me near him. In the light of day, I realized he blamed me. Us. For this. Octavia had done this because Nate had left her. Broken things off. People broke up all the time. This wasn't fair. To react this way. To take another life with your own. She had to be in a very dark place but I was angry at her. For her choice. For what she took. How could she do that? Leave her family behind? I'd not been given a choice. I had to fight to live yet she just threw her life away and that of her child's.

"Do you think someone is making sure he eats?"

Eli walked over and sat at my feet on the edge of the bed. "Yes. Now that I know what happened, what I saw last night makes sense. I think that his dad came here to get him. Didn't want him to drive. Brought the other man to drive his truck home. I watched his dad hug him tightly. I think he's being watched over. He's not alone."

"He has good parents," I said more for my sake than anything. Reminding myself what I knew already.

"I'm glad."

I nodded and finally sat up. "He blames me. He blames us.

What we did. Him breaking up with her because of me. I . . . I kissed him before he broke up with her. Maybe I am to blame. He could hate me and be justified." I dropped my head into my hands. "I just don't understand it. How someone can be so upset that they take their life knowing the devastation they'll leave behind."

Eli let out a deep sigh. "I don't either. But we don't know where her head was. She could have been in a twisted dark place and didn't know how to ask for help. Who to ask."

That wasn't enough for me. Maybe Eli thought she had an excuse but I didn't She just took lives like they weren't meaningful. Like every breath we take isn't a gift. Because it is. I knew that. I knew that every time I saw the sunrise it wasn't something to take for granted. It was something to be thankful for. It wasn't to be tossed away. Life was special. No matter how hard it got it could get better. You had to trust that.

"I know you fought to live, Bliss. You see life as the precious gift it is. I also know that is what you're sitting there battling over in your head. But people have problems. Their brains betray them. They need help maybe even medication. You don't know what her thoughts were when she did it."

For now, I just needed him to stop. I didn't want to hear that. I didn't believe it. The wake of sorrow that her selfish choices made would never heal.

~NATE FINLAY~

I COULD HEAR their voices downstairs. They were all here. Both my sisters. My Uncle Grant, Aunt Harlow and Lila Kate. Aunt Nan, Uncle Cope, Finn, and I could even hear Calla's loud voice. They'd let her out of school today it seems. They were all here for me. It was my family. It's what we did. We were there for each other.

Although I expected this I didn't want it. Having Dad show up last night and drive me home had been what I needed. The fact I was too emotionally fucked up to drive hadn't registered then. But when he and Uncle Grant stepped out of the truck I knew that I wanted them there.

The large group downstairs, I didn't want. I needed to be left alone. They couldn't cheer me up. They didn't understand it all. No one knew what had happened exactly. They were blaming this on Octavia coming off her meds. She dealt with depression. What I hadn't told anyone was that I might have put that rope around her neck.

I knew now she wanted to tell me about the baby. I'd told her I didn't care with my response. All because I loved Bliss York. Love wasn't supposed to cause this. It was supposed to make you happy and all that shit that was downstairs. Married people that I'd grown up watching and wondering if love was that great. Or just a lot of work.

When I finally think maybe they were all on to something, I'm thrown into a nightmare. Fuck being in love. I had wanted easy. I had chosen something more and it screwed up everything. It hurt so many people. It had taken my son. My son. I'd had a son.

But he was gone. Just like his mother. So quickly. So needlessly.

My door opened and mom stepped inside and closed it behind her. The apologetic look on her face told me she knew I didn't want them all here.

"They're worried about you," she said simply.

I understood that. But I still wanted privacy.

"You can come eat with us or I'll bring you up breakfast. But you've got to eat."

Last night she had been out at the truck before I could even step out of it. Like dad she'd wrapped me in her arms. Her face had been wet with tears and her eyes red and swollen. She hadn't said anything but that she loved me.

There had been nothing more to say. She understood me better than anyone. Even dad. Like now. She was quietly coming to check on me. Knowing I wouldn't want to go down there and face them all.

"I'll come down to eat. If I don't they'll all start coming up here." I didn't want to but not eating wasn't happening with Blaire Finlay. She was stubborn.

"I'd like to do a memorial service with just family for him," she said the words so quietly I almost didn't hear her. Him. My son. The one who wasn't given a chance. The pain tore through me again so fiercely I winced. But she was right. We should. He deserved to be remembered. His life acknowledged

"Okay," I replied.

She nodded and tears filled her eyes. She walked over to pull me into her arms again. "He would have been beautiful. Just like you."

I didn't want to think about that now. Maybe one day I'd be able to think of how he would look. What he would have been like. But not now. I wasn't ready. I let my mother grieve in her own way.

She let me go and kissed my cheek. "I love you."

"I love you too."

"Come when you're ready," she told me before turning to leave the room.

I wasn't sure I would be ready in the next year but that wasn't what she meant. She wanted me to come in the next hour. Getting this over with so I could return to my solitude was the best I could do.

Grabbing a tee shirt, I pulled it on to go with the sweat pants I had slept in. I didn't care about my hair or brushing my teeth. If my breath stunk they might keep their distance. I prepared myself for all the well meant love and support I was about to walk into and headed downstairs.

Aunt Nan was talking about Calla getting a bad grade and her threat to pull her out of cheerleading when I walked into the room. They all seemed to notice me at once and the room went silent. No one moved except for Aunt Nan. She immediately got up from her chair and came straight to me. Grabbed my arms and kissed my cheek hard then pulled me tightly into a hug. "You're strong, Nate Finlay. Tough as nails. You're going to hurt in a way I can't imagine but you will make it through. You will find happiness and you will be okay." Her words were said with such conviction I almost believed them.

I hugged her back and whispered a "thanks" even though I didn't think I deserved to ever be okay. When she let me go she turned to my mother. "I'll fix him some coffee while you get his plate ready."

Mom was already working on my food as she nodded.

"Now don't you all stand around here acting like the sound of your voices are going to break him. Talk dammit," Uncle Grant's words would have made me smile if there was a chance I could have.

They all started slowly talking again. Mom put my plate down across from where my dad was sitting with his coffee. He had been silent but his steady gaze had been on me. I looked at him and the solemn expression in his eyes said more than any words. He was worried about me and wanted to fix this but knew he couldn't.

"You sleep?" he asked as I sat down.

"Some."

He nodded and took a drink of his coffee. His eyes shifted to Uncle Grant as he sat down beside me. "Love you, kid," he told me as he squeezed my shoulder.

I knew that. I knew they all did but they were all at a loss of what to say.

Finn stood nervously to the side a few feet away but I saw him watching me. He wasn't sure if he should get closer or what to do. I turned to my younger cousin. "Have a sit," I told him nodding to the chair to my right. "It's okay."

Finn was nineteen now. When he had been born, he'd been a baby that bored me. But soon he had become my little shadow and I liked it. Having him look up to me and mimic me made me feel important. He was the little brother I never had. Although he was much larger than me now. He was the size of his father and Uncle Cope was a big man. He was also quieter like his dad. His sister however was like Aunt Nan. She was chatty and loved attention.

"I'm sorry," Finn said in his deep voice.

"Me too," I replied.

Arms wrapped around my neck from behind. Expensive perfume met my nose then a kiss was pressed to my cheek. She didn't say anything. She didn't have to. That was Ophelia. The sister I had adored until she stole my bedroom and painted it pink. I'd been one angry six-year-old boy. But Phoenix had been born and my parents needed Ophelia's room for the nursery. And I was the oldest so they moved me into the far bedroom. I finally forgave her when she came into my room crying big crocodile tears after they brought Phoenix home from the hospital. She wasn't the baby anymore and she was afraid they'd forget her or give her away.

I reached up and touched her arm. I didn't have to say anything to her. She knew I was glad she was here. We didn't see each other as much anymore and I missed her. Having them all here wasn't as bad as I thought. Their voices all began to grow louder as several conversations took place.

Eating my breakfast, I listened and tried to join in when they wanted me to. But my heart wasn't in it. I wasn't sure I even had one anymore.

Chapter Twenty One

♥ BLISS YORK ♥

WINE WAS GOOD. I liked wine. No, I loved wine. It could possibly be the best thing ever made. Jesus liked the wine. He turned water into wine. The wine is good. Definitely yummy.

I stared at the three empty bottles sitting on the bar while I ate out of the bag of potato chips I had bought when I bought the wine. Shame I was out of the wine. I needed more but I wasn't sure if I left this apartment that I'd find my way back. I would have to walk. I may be drunk but I wasn't stupid. I couldn't drive. Not like this.

A few chips missed my mouth and I watched them fall to the floor. I should pick them up. But I didn't care. Eli would care. I should pick them up for him. Instead I put the bag of chips down and moved to the brownies I had also purchased. Brownies were good. Maybe as good as the wine. But I don't think Jesus ate brownies. No there were never brownies mentioned in Sunday School. I wonder when brownies were created. Should Google it. Find out and celebrate their birthday.

The door closed and I jumped, screamed, and dropped my

brownie. I probably wouldn't pick it up either.

"Bliss?" Eli's voice caught my attention.

"Hello, Eli."

His gaze went from me to the wine bottles and the food I had been consuming all open on the counter.

"You okay? Larissa called and said you didn't show up for work."

Oh, yeah. Work. I wasn't in the mood for work. I had taken off last week because leaving my room had been too much. I'd avoided everyone I could. Then when it was time for me to go to work I drove right passed it went to the grocery store instead and bought wine, chips, brownies, birthday cake, hot wings, and some grapes.

"I was hungry. And thirsty instead," I explained.

"I can see that."

I handed him the box of brownies. "These are good. The have little candies on them instead of nuts. Want one? I drank all the wine but I have food left."

His eyes went wide. "You drank three bottles of wine?"

Sighing I nodded. "Yeah. I should have bought four."

"No, you should have bought one," he said. "Let's stop for the night okay. You've had enough of everything it seems. You won't feel good in the morning. Time you went to bed. You go lay down and I'll bring you a glass of water and an aspirin.

I started to argue that I was still hungry but my stomach rolled and I felt sweaty. "Okay," I agreed and began walking to the bathroom. I didn't feel good. Not at all. My stomach rolled again just as I reached the door to my bathroom and I ran to the toilet hitting my knees with a thud just before it all came back up. One heave after another.

When it finally stopped and all I had was a few dry heaves

I felt Eli behind me. He had my hair in his hand. I wanted to lay down here and started to but a cold washcloth was on my face and it felt nice.

"That will help in the morning. You got it all out now. Let's get you to bed."

I stood up as he picked me up under my arms and staggered into my bedroom. My bed seemed so far away and sleeping on the floor was a good idea. I tried. Eli wouldn't let me though. He forced me to keep walking and when I finally made it across the great ocean of my room I fell down face first. Into soft warmth. My bed.

I'd never been really drunk. Never thrown up because of alcohol. Never slept in my clothes all night with vomit breath. Until now. Opening my eyes hurt. But what was worse was the taste in my mouth. Yuck. Closing my eyes helped with the pain. Didn't help with the nasty in my mouth though.

Voices were in the apartment. Eli wasn't alone. I didn't want to get up and I hoped no one came in here. Last night hadn't been my finest hour. It might have been my lowest one. But for awhile, I was happy. I had food and the alcohol helped with the emptiness and sorrow that I had been trying to live with the past week.

"I told you she's okay, Larissa. Leave her alone." Eli's voice was loud enough for it to be clear through the door.

"She missed work. She's not come out of her room in a week. She's hurting Eli and she needs help. She needs someone to pull her out of it."

Larissa knew. They all knew now. It had made the news. Octavia's father was too well known for it not to. The entertainment world had gone on about her ended relationship with Dean Finlay's grandson. Seeing it had been terrible. Knowing Nate wasn't able to hide and mourn in peace.

My door opened then and I squinted my eyes to see Larissa coming in. She closed the door behind her. "I get that you're hurting. The whole thing is tragic. Terrible and it kills me that you're dealing with this. You of all people should get to live in a happy world where shit don't happen. But it does happen. It hurts. You know that more than anyone. As your friend, I am here to get you out of bed, showered and dressed and out of this place. We are going to get food, walk down the beach, shop, whatever. You aren't staying in here another day."

I wanted to argue but I didn't think I had a chance with her.

"And good for you, getting drunk. Skipping work. And doing the unexpected. It's about time. You can't be perfect, Bliss. No one is."

I wasn't trying to be perfect, was I?

"Up. Come on. You stink like wine and vomit." She pulled my arms and I sat up. "You're the strongest person I've ever met. You're going to be okay. Life is going to go on and you will heal. You'll find that happiness. And he will heal too."

Tears stung my eyes. This wasn't about me. Not about my pain. It was about Nate's. "She killed his son." That was all I could say.

Larissa wrapped me in her arms. "Yeah. She did. He's going to suffer that for a long time. But one day he will find a way to move on. He will always remember but he will heal too."

"I want that for him. He'll never be mine. I'll always be a reminder. That hurts so bad. I don't want him to think of me an immediately remember this."

Larissa squeezed me tightly. "In time you won't remind him of this. You'll remind him of a happier time. One he cherishes."

She was wrong. But I let her say it anyway.

~NATE FINLAY~

A CUP OF coffee appeared in front of me as I sat staring out at the waves crashing on the sand. Tilting my head back, I looked up at Lila Kate. She'd been quiet this week. Not said much at the family gatherings or the memorial. But that was her. She wasn't loud like Calla. She didn't do things to draw attention like Phoenix. And she wasn't striking like Ophelia. She was just . . . well she was just like her mother.

"How are you holding up?" she asked taking the seat beside me. Lila Kate would have been my partner in crime when we were kids if she hadn't been so damn sweet. She was so good and obedient I never could have much fun with her. Cruz Kerrington and I were always into some trouble and Lila Kate was always there worried about us and trying to talk us out of it. We were thrown together from birth. Teasing Lila Kate had been one of our favorite things to do.

That all changed with Cruz kissed Lila Kate when he was thirteen and she was fourteen. Then the next week Cruz was kissing Melanie Harnett. Lila Kate never spoke to him again. Cruz didn't seem to notice. He went through a different girl every week. I knew Lila Kate kissing Cruz had been different than when she kissed me. We hadn't enjoyed the experience. However, it was obvious she didn't feel that way about kissing Cruz.

The one thing that I always noticed though was Lila Kate watched him. For years. He never saw it or her. Cruz was wrapped up in his world. Didn't see much past his next good time. But I saw her. Probably because I often wondered if our parents were right. Maybe we belonged together. Then I would think about how much like a sister she was and throw that idea out fast.

"It sucks," I finally replied to her question.

"Yes, I imagine it does."

Lila Kate didn't have to say a lot. She was just comforting with her silence. I always liked that about her.

"You've got them all worried. Blaire was at mom and dad's today. I walked in the kitchen to see her crying. Mom was talking to her."

That was another thing about Lila Kate, she didn't hold back because she was worried about hurting you. She was sweet and kind but blunt. Honest was probably a better description.

"I don't like making her cry. But I can't pretend that I'm okay."

"I didn't say you could. Just letting you know what's going on."

We sat there for a while drinking our coffee. I knew she wasn't done yet. She was going to say more but was deciding what to say and how to say it. I didn't care to hear anyone's opinion. No one knew what all I had lost. They didn't know there was more. That I loved a woman and had caused this. That although Octavia and my son were dead, I still loved Bliss when that love had been why this happened. Telling anyone that seemed impossible.

At the memorial for my son, I had wanted Bliss there. To stand beside me. To give me comfort. I needed her. Yet I didn't deserve her. There was a grave marked "Baby Finlay" that said I didn't deserve any happiness.

Bliss was happiness for me.

"Who was she? The girl from the letter. ."

No one had asked me that. Octavia's letter had said that she hoped I lived happily with the woman I threw her away for. We had all read the note. Her father made sure I saw it. He blamed me for Octavia getting off her meds. For me turning my back on her. And he should. When she'd wanted to talk I should have let her. Then my son would still have had a chance.

"I love her. I have since I was sixteen years old. But that doesn't matter anymore."

Lila Kate turned her head and I felt her gaze on me. "Why? Because a sick woman acted out of her own darkness? Her own battles? Where were her parents? Why didn't they know she was hurting? She wasn't yours to protect. Y'all had ended things. Letting Octavia's actions determine your choices isn't fair. Not to you or the girl you love."

I didn't have a response to that. I just knew it wasn't that simple. "Not now. . I can't." I replied turning to finally look at her.

She frowned then leaned back in her seat. We drank our coffee and sat in silence for the next hour.

When footsteps sounded on the steps I turned my attention toward them. Cruz appeared from the beach. He'd been running. He was sweating and in his running shorts. He'd come to the memorial but he had been unsure what to say to me. Most had been.

"Hey. Y'all got room for one more?" he asked.

Lila Kate immediately stood up. "I was leaving," then she turned and did just that. Like she always did. When Cruz Kerrington was around she exited. There was no secret that she disliked him. Her actions had made that clear years ago.

"Always could make that girl clear a room. Can't figure out why she hates me so damn much."

I would argue that he was being stupid. That he did know. But in all honesty, I don't think he does. He is too self-absorbed to have noticed.

"You gave a fourteen-year-old Lila Kate her first real kiss then moved on to another girl a week later. While little Lila Kate was in love you were making a legacy as a womanizer for yourself."

Cruz sat down. "Really? She hates me because I kissed her? That was what like eight years ago? That can't be it."

I didn't have the energy to explain it or point it all out. Instead I shrugged. He could believe what he wanted.

"What about you? You making it?"

I was living. "Sure." What else did I say to that?"

"I'm sorry, man. I should have come by before now but I didn't know what to say. Still don't."

There was nothing he could say. "How's working for your dad?" I asked him.

He let out a groan of frustration. "Hard. I miss college."

The Kerrington Country Club would be his one day. He knew it but he also didn't want it. He just didn't have the balls to tell his dad that. He had two younger brothers. Blaze and Zander. He should let one of them have it.

"Do either of your brothers have interest in it?"

He shook his head. "Blaze is off in L.A. still. Trying to be the next Zac Efron. And Zander is planning on the Marines."

I'd seen Blaze on the television nighttime drama he was making a name for himself on. But only once and I hadn't watched the whole show. Phoenix had been watching it and wanted me to see Blaze.

We talked about nothing important and for a few short moments I didn't think about my reality.

Chapter Twenty Two

♥ BLISS YORK ♥

I SHOULD HAVE kept driving. But I didn't. The sign was already taken down and the windows were dark. Nothing there now. It was empty. I sat in my car and thought about the first day I had walked in there and applied for a job. It was just a couple months ago. Yet my world had completely altered since then.

Octavia's sign was gone. There was a "For Lease" poster on the door. The same door I had walked out of and dropped boxes then came face to face with Nate. Who I never expected to see again.

Would this all be different if I hadn't applied for a job here that day? If I'd gone somewhere else and never locked eyes with Nate? Would he have stayed with her, married her, had his son? Tears stung my eyes as I thought of the life he could have had.

It had been three weeks now since he'd left. Not a second went by that I didn't think of him. That I didn't worry about him. That my heart didn't ache for all he was going through. But I couldn't call. I couldn't ask him if he was okay or how he was doing. I could do nothing.

Today I would start my new job. I was going to be the new

director for youth services and marketing at the Sea Breeze Library. Saffron and Holland's mother was a famous author so she had pulled a few strings for me. I didn't know it however until I had gotten the job. My boss had mentioned Blythe Corbin doing a signing because of me getting the position. I'd asked mom if she knew anything about it and she said no. I wasn't sure how Blythe had known I applied.

As much as I enjoyed Live Bay working there wasn't what I wanted to do. I preferred to go there as a customer. Serving my friends was taxing at times. I didn't know how Larissa put up with it.

I started to back out and head to work when Eli's truck pulled up beside me. He had driven by and saw my car and probably thought I was having a break down. I didn't want to get out of my car. It was silly but standing there in front of the store seemed wrong now.

Eli got out of his truck and walked over to get in my passenger side. He didn't say anything at first. Just looked at the store and all its emptiness. There had been so much to happen here in such a short time. Octavia would have been pregnant with his son when I got this job. Had she known? And if she had why not tell Nate?

"Looks sad. Lonely," Eli remarked.

"It does."

"You been here long?"

"No. Just needed to see it."

He sighed. "You seem better."

"I am better. My heart will always hurt for Nate. For his pain. But my life will also go on. I can't just quit. Life is a gift."

"You know that better than anyone."

I hadn't meant that others didn't know it. But yes, after facing death you look at life differently. It changes you.

"Do you think he will ever come back here? That I'll ever

see him again?"

"Don't know. Maybe. I hope. For your sake."

He meant that.

"I miss him. I just don't know if seeing him again would be too much. It may be best that the night on the beach was it. My last memory of him. Eventually I'll move on but I don't think my heart ever truly will."

"Bliss, he'll come back one day. I may not have lost a child. And I may not feel like someone ended their life because of me. But I am a man. I know how we think. And I know if I was in love with someone like you I'd come back. I'd have to. That being said, you can't put your life on hold. When you're ready. Date again. Enjoy life."

I wasn't sure he was right. Part of me hoped he was the other part prayed he wasn't. I just didn't want to live waiting on a man to return that never did. For now, it didn't matter. I wasn't moving on anytime soon. I had friends and a job. And I had my memories.

"Want me to bring you lunch today?"

No. I didn't want to eat. "Yes. That would be nice." It was time I pushed through my sadness. Tried to find joy again.

"I'll be there with greasy burgers around noon."

"No. Not those. Anything else." I'd had greasy burgers my first day at Octavia's. The day Nate arrived. I couldn't eat those now.

"Okay. Then I'll choose," he said not having to ask why.

He got back out of the car and went and got in his truck. But he didn't leave until I cranked my car. Once I pulled out he followed behind me. Eli had been patient and understanding through all this. Being at home with him was quiet and easier than it would have been to go to my parents. They'd hover. I didn't want that. I had needed to drink too much wine, eat icing out of a jar, and vomit a couple of times.

He had held my hair for me and wiped my face and made

sure my drunk ass got in bed. He was the best kind of friend there was. The one that you've had forever and knows what you need.

I needed to stop by Live Bay and pick up my last paycheck but I'd do that tonight after work. Eli hadn't mentioned rent and I'd forgotten. This morning it hit me and I needed to get it to him. It wasn't like me to forget something like that but these past few weeks I had been very unBlisslike.

I picked up my phone after I pulled into the library parking lot and texted Eli.

"I have the rent money. I'll get it to you. Sorry I forgot."

I waited a moment for a response.

"Good. I would hate to have to kick you out on the street."

I laughed. I hadn't laughed in weeks. Three to be exact.

Smiling at my phone I was thankful I could laugh again. I hoped that Nate could too. I hope he found things to smile about. Things that brightened his day. And that eventually our time together wasn't a bad memory. I wanted to think he could think of me again and smile. Not today. But eventually.

Stepping out of the car I grabbed my purse and laptop and headed inside to the start of something new. Again.

~NATE FINLAY~

THERE WAS A champagne colored Bentley parked outside my parent's house. I hadn't been by to visit them in a few days. Once I moved back to my house, I'd put distance between me and everyone. It was worrying my mother according to Ophelia and my dad who had called to inform me. Before my dad showed up at my house to kick my ass for not going to see mom I decided to go visit her.

Mom had company and I wasn't in the mood for visiting

anyone else. But I was here now and needed to get it over with. Facing other people was eventually going to happen. Unless I bought a deserted island and moved there.

I didn't knock. I never did. This had been my home for 19 years. I walked inside and followed the voices. They were in the living room. As I stepped inside my ears heard the voice of the guest and although I had only been around he woman few times I knew who it was.

My eyes went from Octavia's stepmother to my mother. Why was she here?

"Nate, I'm glad you're here. "Saylor is actually here to see you," my mom said. As if I would want to see anyone related to Octavia.

"Why?" was my only response.

"Because she has some information she felt you should hear. I agree with her."

My mother wasn't one to listen to something she didn't believe. Because of that I remained in the room. What I wanted to do was head for the door and not look back.

"Sit down, Nate," mom said. Not "do you want to have a seat?" she was telling me I was staying and listening. Which meant I was staying and listening.

I did as I was ordered but I took the seat closest to the escape route. If she began talking about things I didn't want to discuss I was gone. They both needed to be prepared for that.

"Saylor called me yesterday and asked if she could come speak with you. I told her she could come talk to me first. After listening to her I was ready to call you. I see that your father beat me to it." She turned to Saylor. "Go ahead."

Saylor was once a lingerie model. She'd met Octavia's dad during a photo shoot she was in for his department store. They'd fallen in lust. He began fucking her and his wife found out. That marriage ended. This one then came a month after. She was still young and beautiful just past the lingerie modeling age. Octavia and Saylor had gotten along. Octavia just didn't really care who her father was with as long as he gave her money.

"I know what you've been told. What you've been blamed for. At first I thought the same thing. But then a few things happened that made me question what the letter from Octavia said. Sure she had issues. We all knew that. She was spoiled beyond repair. However, when a psychiatrist came to the funeral and told us how sorry he was for our loss and that he'd tried to help Octavia the past couple of years the best he could her father demanded his records or he'd have him accused of something and his license to practice taken away. So he got the records.

Octavia was molested as a child by a close friend of her father's. It went on for years until Octavia was old enough to get away from him. Two years ago, she paid a hit man to kill him. The disappearance of Vincent Brooklyn is now solved. He's been dead for two years and his body is at the bottom of the Mississippi River."

She paused and I tried to wrap my head around this. I had been to the man's house before with her father. When he went missing Octavia been truly upset or acted like it. She had called him Uncle Vincent.

"The guilt of his murder was making her depression more severe. She was withdrawing and working on the store as a way to distract herself. She knew she was pregnant for three months. She was considering abortion and saying she didn't want to be a mother. Months before you broke things off. What she wanted to talk to you about was she needed to confess her crime. She thought that telling you everything would ease her guilt. She never planned to tell you she was pregnant. She wasn't going to keep the baby. Her abortion date had been scheduled. You are not the reason she hung herself or killed your child. She was never even going to tell you she was pregnant."

All I could do was sit there. It was once again like I was hearing a horror story that wasn't real. This time I didn't have guilt on my shoulders. But the horror was all the same. Octavia had lived a much darker life inside her head than I imagined.

She'd suffered and mentally she wasn't stable. She never had been. I had missed that. Thinking her indifference and distance was a good thing. She'd been that way to protect her secrets.

It didn't change the fact I had lost my son. I would have lost him anyway and never even known it. She was never going to let me have him. She didn't want a child. She'd said that often.

Standing up I walked out. I couldn't speak. I couldn't ask questions. I just needed to leave. Be alone. My mother didn't come running after me. She understood.

I climbed back into my truck and drove. I ignored my phone. I'd call them back. I just drove. I drove until the town changed. Until the scenery became something else familiar. Until I was parked outside my grandpop's bar.

Sitting there I let the facts measure up in my head. I was able to let go of the self-blame. Move on from the guilt. I mourned the lives lost that didn't have to be. For the sickness that causes people to act in a way that ruins lives and often ends them. I mourned the woman she could have been if she hadn't been abused. I mourned the life my son could have had.

But I no longer blamed me. I was free of that guilt. My choices didn't make Octavia take her life and the life of my unborn son. Her choices and emotional damage had. I'd missed that. Yes. I hadn't realized she was hiding pain but then we'd never been connected. I'd called that easy. When, in reality, it was wrong.

I wanted what my parents had. I wanted that connection. I wanted a life with a woman I loved. That I could share with. The other way no longer felt easy. It was lonely. It was empty.

I wanted Bliss.

Opening my truck door, I got out and headed inside. My Grandpop had been worried about me. Called several times. Mom had told him I needed space not to come. Now I needed to plan. Decide how I would approach Bliss. She hadn't heard from me in two months. I didn't know what she was doing or if she was dating. The way we felt . . . the way it had been I didn't want to think she could move on so quickly. But I owed her more. And I wanted to give it all to her. I was ready to deserve her. Whatever I had to do I was willing to do it.

Chapter Twenty Three

TODAY HAD BEEN a success. The turn out for the first Teen Day at the library had been bigger than I hoped. One hundred and eleven teens came to meet the author and play the trivia games we had set up for them. I was happily humming to myself as I finished cleaning up the area we had held the event when the Media director, Matthew Goodwin, came walking into the room. He was six foot tall with dark brown hair and pretty green eyes. He had a definite nerdy vibe with his glasses and technical side but he was attractive. He pulled it off.

I could tell he was interested in me by his daily flirting. It was subtle. Almost shy like. If there hadn't been a Nate in my life. If I hadn't fallen in love with him all over again just months ago then maybe Matthew would have been fun. Maybe we could have made it work. But there had been a Nate. And my heart wasn't ready.

"Great event," Matthew said with his straight white teeth smile.

"Yes it was. I couldn't be more pleased with the turn out."

"Never had an event here so successful."

That fact made me beam with pride. I may have gotten this

job because of Blythe but being successful at it was important to me. I wanted them to be glad they hired me.

"I'm glad tomorrow is Sunday. I need a lazy day at home."

"I can imagine after today. What about tonight? You headed home?"

I had thought about going to Live Bay. Having a drink, visiting with friends, being normal. Things I rarely did anymore.

"Not sure," I replied honestly.

"Want to go get a drink?"

Here it was. The question. It wasn't a date. Just drinks. I could invite him to Live Bay. We may enjoy each other's company. It could be good for me.

"I was thinking of going to see some friends at Live Bay. You want to come with me?"

The smile was back on his face. I wished I felt that excited about this. Instead it felt wrong. I couldn't back out now.

"Sounds fun."

Great. He was coming. Okay. I asked him, now I just had to get through it.

"I'm headed out the door. You ready?" I tried to sound happy.

"Yeah, already closed up my section."

We started for the door and my brain was racing trying to come up with an excuse to cancel. I didn't want to do this. I wanted to go home now. Be alone. I had changed my mind. I started to say something when my eyes locked on the man standing at my car. I stopped walking.

He was here.

Or I was delusional.

Could be that I had lost my mind.

"Do you know him?" Matthew asked and I nodded. My voice wasn't working. Words weren't there. If Matthew saw him too then I hadn't lost my mind. He was actually there. At my car.

"Are you okay? Need me to have him leave?"

This time I just shook my head no. Still words weren't work-ing. Nate took a step in my direction and I was unsure what to do. Was he here to tell me something? To see me? To rip open the wounds that were still fresh?

"I can't . . . I have to . . ." I was trying to tell Matthew I wouldn't be going to Live Bay. Because after this encounter I would need more bottles of wine and cake while I once again nursed the pain.

"If you don't want to see that guy I can make him leave," Matthew said. He sounded as if he believed he could. I knew he couldn't. Didn't matter. I wanted to see Nate. Hear his voice. Know that he was okay. Even if wine and a lot of calories followed.

"I need to see him. I won't be going to Live Bay tonight." There I had said words. They came out.

Matthew paused then replied. "Okay. Well, I'll see you Mon-day."

Again, I just nodded.

Taking the first step in Nate's direction my heart squeezed and fluttered. Knowing this wasn't going to be easy I still wanted to be near him. He looked thinner. There were dark circles under his eyes. But he was still beautiful. The most beautiful man I'd ever seen. I was positive he always would be.

"I should have called first," he said when I was close enough to him.

"It's okay. It's . . . good to see you."

His eyes shifted to Matthew who was taking his time leaving. "Is he, are y'all dating?"

The pain in his eyes as he asked that told me he didn't want me to be. That felt good. Knowing he wanted me still. That even after all the bad he still cared. I wasn't a terrible mistake. I didn't want to be.

"No. He's a friend. A coworker."

Nate's gaze was back on me. He let out what could only be described as a sigh of relief. "How long have you been at this job? It fits you better than Live Bay did."

"A few weeks. Maybe a month," I wasn't sure. My head was swimming with questions.

"Can we go somewhere? Talk? Or do you have plans?"

Didn't he realize I'd drop any plans for him? Had I not made myself clear two months ago when we had slept together. I didn't do that lightly.

"Yes."

He nodded to his truck. "I'll drive. Come with me."

I walked beside him and he opened the passenger door. He was standing so close I could smell his cologne as I walked past him to climb inside. Even after all the pain all I could think about in that moment was burying my head in his neck and inhaling. Feeling his warm body against mine. If just for a moment. I wanted that before he left again.

The door closed once I was inside. He walked around the front of the truck with the same easy cool swagger he always had. Little things like that I had missed. He was here now. I had to soak it all in. His voice, his smell, the way he walked. All of it. Things I hadn't realized would be gone so soon before.

~NATE FINLAY~

"*WHEN YOU MEET a girl that you still love once she's a woman then you don't give that up. .*" Grandpop's words replayed over and over in my ears. He was right. I'd fallen in love with the girl and the woman she had become owned me. My happiness was with her. Life without her wasn't something I ever had to face again.

Fuck easy. Life wasn't easy. Love wasn't easy. Not the real thing anyway. The real thing hurt like hell and gave you the best moments of your life.

I parked the truck outside the building her condo and my grandpop's was in. This was where I'd left her. This was where I would now fight for her . . . for us.

"Let's go to my Grandpop's. He's working and we can have privacy."

"Okay," she agreed.

We hadn't spoken in the short ride over here. I was going over all I needed to say in my head. Now I feared what she had been going over in her head. Was she ready to get her closure?

I opened the door to Grandpop's condo and stood back so she could go inside. She looked nothing like any librarian I had ever seen. The yellow shorts, white sandals with thin sexy heels had to distract every man who came in to check out a book. Or teenagers. She was working in the teen department Larissa had said when I went by Live Bay looking for her.

"You want a drink?" I asked.

She shook her head. "No."

Me either. "How have you been?"

She frowned. "Okay. What about you?"

"Life has sucked. Dark, ugly and painful. But something did change. That's why I'm here." Where to even begin with this.

"What changed?"

She knew I had left because I blamed myself. I made that clear.

"Octavia's stepmother came to see me. They found something out about Octavia's death. There were things they didn't know. A secret no one knew and guilt that was eating Octavia alive. She was seeing a psychiatrist who came to the funeral. Octavia's father had the power to demand to see the records from her visits and he found the real reason behind Octavia's suicide."

Talking about my son was hard. Knowing he never had a chance at life in the beginning hurt. She'd never intended to let him live. I wanted to scream from the unfairness until my chest didn't ache. The hole it left behind would always be there. It wasn't going away.

"She was sexually abused as a child. From a family friend. A man she referred to as her uncle. She had him killed once she was an adult and the guilt was eating at her. Even if the man deserved to die from sexually abusing a child. She couldn't live with the secret."

Bliss covered her mouth with one hand and tears filled her eyes. "Oh my god," she breathed. "Oh, Nate. I'm so sorry."

"She had an abortion scheduled for later that month. She never intended to let our child live. She wasn't going to tell me about him. She didn't want him."

The tears on her face were sincere. She hurt for me. For Octavia and for my son.

"The damage he caused her . . . I lived through a hell of my own but nothing like that. I had support and love while I fought a disease. She had no one. She faced a monster as a child and there was no love and support to stand with her. That's heartbreaking."

I hadn't thought of it that way. Bliss was right. Octavia had been through a private hell alone. Her mental sickness was something that might have been avoided if she'd had love and support around her. But she'd been alone in it all. A detached woman who needed money and success. Who was looking for something to fill her void.

We stood there in silence. I would always regret not knowing Octavia's pain and being able to help her. Even if I had known I wasn't sure I could have helped but I would have tried.

Bliss wiped at her tears again.

"I love you," the words came so easily. Words I should have

said already. That I should have said the moment those boxes fell and she was standing there staring at me with those big blue eyes. Because even then deep down I had known the truth.

She took a step toward me. "You do?"

I had been hoping for an "I love you too" but her question and the surprise on her face made me smile anyway.

"Yeah. I always have. The girl you were and the woman you became."

She let out a sob and then she was there. Against me burying her face in my neck. I hadn't meant to make her cry like this but I was hoping they were good tears.

"Bliss," I said touching her hair gently with my hand to comfort her. "That wasn't supposed to make you cry."

She let out a laugh then and lifted her tear streaked face. "I'm sorry. It was too much all at once. The sadness then this. I wasn't expecting this."

"You weren't expecting me to tell you I loved you?" I asked wanting to clarify.

She nodded. "Yes. I love you. I love you so much. But I didn't think . . . I just thought you liked me a lot. But that we were done."

"Liked you a lot?" I asked grinning.

She pressed her lips together as she tried not to smile. "Yes."

"It goes well beyond a lot."

She let out a gentle sigh and closed her eyes. "I feel like I shouldn't be happy. What you came to tell me is so sad. How can I be happy?"

I understood. But I had mourned. In the end, I couldn't have changed anything. "I'll always wonder about my son. He has a piece of my heart now. That will never change. But I want to have a life with joy in it. I want to experience how complicated and hard times feel knowing I'm facing them with you. I want it all, Bliss. As long as I get to spend it with you."

Again she buried her head in my neck and wrapped her arms around me. "Me too."

I held her as we stood there in silence. This was our beginning. The other times had been our prologue. But the real story would start now.

Chapter Twenty Four

♥ BLISS YORK ♥

THE SUN WAS barely breaking through the blinds when I opened my eyes. Nate was asleep beside me. We had eaten in last night and talked about things. I asked all my questions and he seemed to want to tell me. Then we kissed until our clothes were gone and made love in the bed for hours. It had been slow and sweet. Naughty words hadn't been needed.

Watching him sleep peacefully with his arm thrown over me was like a dream. One I had a million times and never expected to experience. I reached over and brushed the hair from his eyes. He was mine. After all these years Nate Finlay was mine.

But for how long?

I'd asked him questions last night now wondering had it been to avoid talking to him about me. My past. My illness. I had avoided it because I didn't want him to see me as the sick girl. If we were going to have a chance at a real relationship I had to talk to him about what all I went through. How it affected my body. Especially now. He'd created a child that he never got to hold. If we stayed together he'd never get to create another one. My body didn't work properly. I'd lost parts of me in the treatments.

I moved to get up quietly so I wouldn't disturb him and pulled his discarded shirt on before going to the kitchen for coffee. Nate said he loved me. Everything he did and said last night also said he loved me. He wanted us to work. Keeping it a secret about what all my body went through especially the fact it couldn't bear children was a lie. I wouldn't lie to him.

The fear that in the end he'd leave me for someone whose body wasn't broken was strong but it was a truth I had to face now. Waiting until later was unfair to both of us. I had come to terms with the fact that I would become a mother by adoption and I was good with it. I wanted to give a child a family. I wanted to love it and raise it. And I knew one day I would adopt more than one child.

After I poured a cup of coffee I sat with my feet curled up under me on the sofa and looked out the window. It wasn't a beach view but the early morning sun danced on the world outside. It was peaceful. Full of promise.

"You left me in bed. Our first morning as a real couple and you left me."

I turned to see Nate standing there shirtless in a pair of boxer briefs. His hair was still mused from last night and his eyes heavy from sleep. A man should not look that good. It was unfair to the females of the world.

"I didn't want to disturb you."

He cocked one eyebrow. "Were you still naked?"

I nodded.

"Then I would have preferred you disturb me. Next time crawl on top of me."

I laughed into my coffee cup. I wanted this so much. But first he had to know.

"I need to tell you something."

His teasing smirk faded. "You look serious. That makes me nervous."

I could drag this out and explain everything but I wanted to say it. Let him process it and figure out if we had a future. One past dating and enjoying each other. One where we grew old together. He may not want to adopt. After losing his son he may need another child with his blood. His smile. A part of him.

"I can't have children. The chemotherapy ruined that part of me." There I said it. He would be reminded I was sick. That I hadn't always looked like this. That I wasn't completely whole.

"Okay," he said walking over to me. He sat down beside me and pulled my legs into his lap. "How do you feel about that?"

What? He was asking me how I felt? I'd known this for a long time. He was the one that needed to adjust and decide how he felt about it. I answered his question anyway. "I'm going to adopt when I'm ready to have kids. A child doesn't have to grow inside me to be mine."

He nodded. "Agreed. Well it wouldn't have grown inside me anyway but I agree with you. I wouldn't love a child any less because they didn't have my blood in their veins. I like the idea we would give a child a home that needed one. That we would love it and raise it the way our parents did us."

I was going to cry again. I had cried a lot the past twenty-four hours. "You really mean that?"

"Hell yeah I mean that," He tugged me closer and I clutched my cup with both hands to keep the little bit of coffee left from spilling. "All I need is you. If I have you I'm happy. Raising a child with you will make me happy. Our baby doesn't have to come from us to be ours."

I sat the cup down beside the sofa. Then promptly threw

myself into his lap wrapping my arms around his neck and peppered kisses all over his face. "I love you more now and I didn't think that was possible."

He chuckled. "Good. I need to get you to love me so damn much you can't ever let me go."

"You succeeded."

He slid a hand under his shirt I was wearing. "How about I show you exactly how much I love you."

"That's not love. That's lust."

He lowered his head to kiss the inside of my thigh. "No baby this is love. Real motherfucking love. I love your pussy. Trust me."

I burst into laughter until his mouth pressed just at the top of my thigh. I went silent and held my breath until his tongue trailed to flick over my swollen clit. I liked this form of love too. I was good with him loving several parts of me.

Because right now I really loved his tongue. A lot. A loved it a whole lot.

"Nate," I panted.

"Hmmm," he said as he continued between my legs.

"Fuck me, please." He paused and lifted his head to look up at me.

Then he moved. So quickly that he was inside me in seconds. "Fuck," he groaned. "I get to come inside you."

"Yes," I replied.

"Goddamn this just got better and I didn't know it could."

Lifting my legs, he sunk deep inside. This was my fairytale. All little girls have them. They normally have a prince and a castle. Until they grow up, then their fairytale becomes something different. Mine was a silver eyed, dirty mouthed, big hearted, man with a magical penis.

~NATE FINLAY~

DINNER WITH HER parents. She had tried to talk me out of going when her mother had called and invited me. But I wanted to meet them. The people who raised her and the brothers she talked so much about. These people would one day be my family too.

The man that opened the door was about my height with dark hair and Bliss's blue eyes. He regarded me with a serious expression then held out his hand. "Cage York, glad you could come."

I shook his hand and I was pretty damn sure he was trying to crush the bones in my hand. This was his warning without Bliss knowing. I wouldn't tell on him later. I got it. Bliss was his only girl. He'd been by her side while she fought for her life. He was protective. I'd just have to prove to him he could trust me.

"Let them in, Cage," a woman who looked exactly what I imagine Bliss would look one day said as she came to the door and shoved her husband over. "You didn't have to meet them at the door. Bliss doesn't have to knock. This is her home."

Cage grunted but his scowl stayed in place. Her mother rolled her eyes at him then smiled at us. "We are thrilled y'all are here. Cord and Clay even canceled their plans for this. They wanted to meet you."

"Yeah, because I wanted to make sure you understood who you'd be dealing with if you hurt my sister," a tall but lanky version of Cage York came to the door. He was frowning like his father.

"Oh for god's sake y'all move so we can get inside or I'm taking him and we are leaving." Bliss said as she took my arm and pulled me inside with her. Then she paused and stood on her tip toes to kiss the lanky boy. "Glad you stayed, Cord. Love you," she said.

He kept his warning glare on me. "Love you too."

That was sweet. There were three of these boys and a dad. I had to convince them all I'd do right by her. And I didn't mind at all.

"You finally brought home a man. I'm impressed," another dark haired blue eyed boy said. This one was even younger than the last.

"Nate, this is Clay my youngest brother. The rude one was Cord he's the middle," she looked around. "Where is Cruz?"

About that time the exact younger version of her father walked in the room. His shoulders were wide. His hair was slightly long and he had a shot gun in his hands. This was getting entertaining.

"I'm just cleaning my gun," he said his eyes locked on me.

"Oh good lord y'all are ridiculous," her mother said. Then she turned to me.

"Excuse my boys. I'm Eva, and this is our crazy household. Bliss never brought boys home so they're not handling it well. They will adjust."

"Don't apologize. I have two younger sisters and I get it. I may have to try that shot gun move with one of their dates."

The oldest one tried to hid his grin but he failed.

"Go put the gun up and y'all help me get the table set," Eva ordered and no one questioned her. The youngest started to act like he didn't hear her and kept his head down looking at his phone.

Cage cleared his throat and the boys head jerked up. Looked at his dad and was out of his seat immediately.

"I like them," I told her under my breath.

"They aren't normally insane."

"They love you."

She smiled then. That smile that made her face light up. It curled just slightly and her eyes would shine with pleasure. "Yeah they do."

"Maybe we could just get boys. No girls so I don't have to do this one day," I suggested.

She laughed then and shook her head. "No way. I grew up with all these boys. I want a girl too."

I would let her get five girls if it made her happy. "Okay fine you win."

"They're whispering and grinning all silly like. Makes me want to vomit," Clay said as he put glasses of ice on the table.

"Shut your stupid mouth," Cruz said glaring at his brother.

"That's enough. We have company please don't embarrass your sister she may never bring him back," her mother said.

"You hunt?" Cage asked me.

"No sir." I hoped that didn't mean I was out before I even got a chance to get in.

"Good. Me either."

I glanced down at Bliss who was smiling at her father. Maybe a girl wouldn't be so bad after all. Sisters were pains in the ass. But a daughter would be different.

"You surf?" Cage then asked.

"Yes sir."

"I like him," he declared. "Have a seat boy. Tell me about yourself."

"Daddy, be nice."

"Hell, Bliss. I'm being nice. It was your crazy ass brother who brought out your granddad's shotgun. Not me."

"I was cleaning it," Cruz interjected.

"Sure you were boy. Sure you were," Cage said with an amused smirk. "Boys love their sister. So you got two sisters huh? What about your parents? Married? Divorced? Lesbians?"

"Jesus, Daddy!"

"CAGE!" Bliss and her mother both reacted at once.

"I'm just asking. If he's parents are lesbians then I don't care. Hell he can have two dads for all I care. I'm just being friendly getting to know the boy."

I liked this man. My dad would too.

"I have a mom and a dad. Still married. And the two sisters."

He nodded. "Know any lesbians?"

"God help me," Eva said as she sat food down at the table.

"As a matter of fact I do," I replied.

He nodded. "What about STD's? You got any of them?"

I laughed. Couldn't help it this time. The man was great.

"Daddy I swear I am about to take him and leave."

Cage held up both hands. "Okay. Okay, fine. I'll stop asking him questions."

"Thank you," Bliss and Eva said in unison.

"Damn I was hoping he was going to ask more about the lesbians," Cord said.

Bliss picked up a roll from the table and threw it at his head.

Sitting back in my seat I looked over at her and smiled. I liked it here. Her family. They were a lot like mine. I could see why she was the person she was today. I'd ask her to marry me soon. Because I couldn't wait much longer. I wanted all this with her. The works. Every complicated beautiful moment of it.

ABBI GLINES

ABBI GLINES IS a #1 New York Times, USA Today, and Wall Street Journal bestselling author of the Rosemary Beach, Sea Breeze, Vincent Boys, Existence, and The Field Party Series . She never cooks unless baking during the Christmas holiday counts. She believes in ghosts and has a habit of asking people if their house is haunted before she goes in it. She drinks afternoon tea because she wants to be British but alas she was born in Alabama. When asked how many books she has written she has to stop and count on her fingers. When she's not locked away writing, she is reading, shopping (major shoe and purse addiction), sneaking off to the movies alone, and listening to the drama in her teenagers lives while making mental notes on the good stuff to use later. Don't judge.

You can connect with Abbi online in several different ways. She uses social media to procrastinate.

www.abbiglines.com
www.facebook.com/abbiglinesauthor
twitter.com/AbbiGlines
www.instagram.com/abbiglines
www.pinterest.com/abbiglines

Other titles by
Abbi Glines

ROSEMARY BEACH SERIES

Fallen Too Far

Never Too Far

Forever Too Far

Rush Too Far

Twisted Perfection

Simple Perfection

Take A Chance

One More Chance

You We're Mine

Kiro's Emily

When I'm Gone

When You're Back

The Best Goodbye

Up In Flames

SEA BREEZE SERIES

Breathe

Because of Low

While It Lasts

Just For Now

Sometimes It Lasts

Misbehaving

Bad For You

Hold On Tight

Until The End

THE FIELD PARTY SERIES
Until Friday Night
Under the Lights
After the Game (Coming August 22, 2017)

ONCE SHE DREAMED
Once She Dreamed (Part 1)
Once She Dreamed (Part 2)

THE VINCENT BOYS SERIES
The Vincent Boys
The Vincent Brothers

EXISTENCE TRILOGY
Existence (Book 1)
Predestined (Book 2)
Leif (Book 2.5)
Ceaseless (Book 3)

CPSIA information can be obtained
at www.ICGtesting.com
Printed in the USA
LVOW11s0923110617

537714LV00003B/558/P